D0422666

Bless the Thief

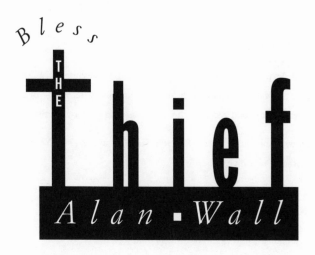

Bless the Thief

Alan · Wall

novel

Crown Publishers, Inc.

NEW YORK

Copyright © 1997 by Alan Wall

All rights reserved. No part of this book may be reproduced or transmitted in any form
or by any means, electronic or mechanical, including photocopying, recording, or by any
information storage and retrieval system, without permission in writing from the publisher.

Published by Crown Publishers, Inc., 201 East 50th Street, New York, New York 10022.
Member of the Crown Publishing Group.

Random House, Inc. New York, Toronto, London, Sydney, Auckland
www.randomhouse.com/

CROWN and colophon are trademarks of Crown Publishers, Inc.

Originally published in Great Britain in 1997 by Martin Secker & Warburg Limited,
20 Vauxhall Bridge Road, London SW1V 2SA,
and Auckland, Melbourne, Singapore, and Toronto

Printed in the United States of America

Design by Lynne Amft

Library of Congress Cataloging-in-Publication Data
Wall, Alan.
   Bless the thief / Alan Wall. — 1st ed.
   (alk. paper)
   I. Title.
 PR6073.A415B57   1998
   823'.914—dc21   97-39839
 ISBN 0-609-60158-X

 10 9 8 7 6 5 4 3 2 1

First American Edition

Contents

With fire our life begins, the great
harsh gift of the sun. And many believe that it's
with fire our life will end.
ISAAC LENAU, *Marginalia,* 147

■

Bless the thief for he lightens your burden.
ALFRED DELAQUAY

Bless the Thief

1

Grimshaw

And lifting up a fearful eye
To view what fire was near
A pretty Babe all burning bright
Did in the air appear . . .
ROBERT SOUTHWELL, "The Burning Babe"

ALMOST AS SOON AS I LEARNED TO SAY DADDY, TO COVER THE
silence into which my father vanished, I learned to say hydrogen too.
The subjects were always connected, it seemed: fatherhood and the
flammability of that pervasive gas. He had died on May 6, 1937, so they
told me; and not at home in bed murmuring his patriarch's blessings
either. He was one of the thirty-three in the *Hindenburg* who came out
screaming when that great pod burst. At Lakehurst, New Jersey. You've
seen the pictures, I would imagine. As the lit seed falls to earth and the
commentator starts to weep. No one's ever been sure what caused it.
Maybe the static electricity after the thunderstorm. Anyhow the hydrogen went up and my old man came down in flames. The seed *he'd* left
behind was me, just trying myself on for size in his wife's womb. That
was in Parsippany, also New Jersey.

So in my boy's room I assembled information, illustrations, models;
learned how it had been christened by Lavoisier two centuries before.
That its atomic number was one. That it was the lightest and most rudimentary of the elements and that it made up three-quarters of the universe. Matter at its simplest had wasted my father, scorched him through

to his bones. The fire ate his skin and swallowed his heart. Where had he gone back to so swiftly before I'd even come to see him?

I stared at the geometric models of my atoms and came to understand that most of us in any case is space, vacuity. We're largely the emptiness time needs to travel on through. And if you burn up in time do you remain then still in time? Is memory time's reversal or its fulfillment?

■

His picture smiled serenely out from several shelves. He looked happy enough, locked in the instant of those exposures, hugging my mother. An Englishman, a scientist. That's all I was told. The key to my future lay in those few words. For when Mr. Terry Quinn arrived at the threshold of my mother's affections, I was then informed of my father's plans as to who I must grow up to be, and where I'd have to go to be it.

My mother had moved back to the States upon my father's death and I was born in her parents' house. My first years were spent in its bland New Jersey comfort. But now it seemed I was to attend the Robert Southwell School on the edge of Ilkley Moor in Yorkshire, England, as my father had before me. It was the first I'd heard of it. They said it had been stipulated in his will, and the finances to enable it thereby provided. Without Mr. Quinn and his amorous regard for my remaining parent, I think my father's will might have been quietly forgotten. Still, once I'd landed on that northern moorside, I soon forgot about the pair of them. Or thought I did. I've never truly forgotten anything in my life. This is one of the curses I shall try to flee in the forthcoming years, the forthcoming pages.

Southwell was Catholic, cold, and gray. Postwar England was Protestant, cold, and gray. They seemed glad to have won the war but surprised to be still receiving the bills. I'd arrived thinking *we'd* won the war but learned to keep my mouth shut after my first bloody nose. *They* won the war—we only arrived at the end to join the celebrations. And drop a couple of bombs on Japan.

The school had been built in 1882 out of funds provided by Jamie Enright, a mill owner from Bradford whose yarn-spinning technique made him a wealthy man. Unlike most of his fellow industrialists, he was a Roman Catholic, and decided to direct some of his wealth toward the education of his coreligionists.

Southwell was made of millstone grit and bells. The stone held firm against the weather, and the bells divided time into waking and sleeping, eating and running, praying and study. I still hear those bells sometimes when I close my eyes.

Dr. Grimshaw was headmaster, and on the morning of the first day of term he made it plain why we were assembled before him. He was a tall, thin man with a residue of gray hair, about sixty years of age. His angular gestures were all made through the gown he invariably wore. He clutched the lectern and fixed his blue eyes on us, his stare seemingly alighting on each face in turn with vivid disbelief.

"Welcome to the Robert Southwell School here in Ilkley. Welcome to history. Our history. Your history. Don't imagine for a moment, boys, that you escape history when you come to the edge of these moors, the edge of this world.

"Robert Southwell: I suppose it's possible that some of you gathered here don't even know who that great man was. A martyr for the old faith when the rest of this country apostatized in the sixteenth century . . ."

By now my attention was wandering. My eyes had started meeting the walls and climbing the ceiling. There was what I would later come to call a hammerbeam roof with angels carved on the brackets. The windows stared grandly out onto the sky from decorated tracery. I understood, I think, in my primitive way that this building did not merely want to contain me, it also wanted to say something to me. It would take me into its corners and whisper something urgently. . . . But by now Dr. Grimshaw's voice was growing urgent too.

"You will be taught about Shakespeare's England in your English and history classes. You will learn of the splendors of that time—properly so, for it was a time of splendor. But as you meditate upon that golden age of Elizabeth, we will also teach you to think of the other side of that splendor. For we *are* the other side of that splendor.

"Before his final martyrdom the poet and priest Robert Southwell was captured and tortured by the unspeakable Richard Topcliffe—Sir Richard Topcliffe, no less—who was an intimate of Her Majesty, Queen Elizabeth. Indeed this pursuivant did nothing without her permission and letters are extant that he wrote to her, in which he jokes filthily of the pains he inflicted.

"It was here in this county that the Pilgrimage of Grace began—that brave protest against the abandonment of the old religion by a bloody and lewd king. The noblemen who instigated it were first tricked and then butchered by men for whom the notion of honor was nothing but an occasion for laughter.

"Six miles upriver from here stand the ruins of Bolton Abbey. It was an Augustinian house of prayer until looted and passed to the dukes of the day—for their profit and personal aggrandizement. Those same lords have subsequently done everything in their power to make the burden of those attached to the old faith in these islands as onerous and penal as might be. If the purchase of their loyalty was expensive, it was also effective.

"You are now that remnant. That discomfiture has now fallen to you. You are what dissolution and so-called reformation could neither dissolve nor reform away. You are here to be fitted with Saint Patrick's breastplate, and if it doesn't immediately fit, then you will have to change your shape until it does. We'll help you—not with the rack they used on the English martyrs, but with the teaching of Christ.

"You are only here for a time, just as we are only here on earth for a time. 'Time cannot exist without a soul to count it,' said Aristotle. He might have added that it wouldn't have any purpose without a soul to count it. For time is the medium in which we grow gracious. It exists so that souls may find God. Even that great heretic William Blake understood how time is the mercy of eternity. You will redeem the time you spend here—willingly, I hope. But if unwillingly, you will still redeem it. You have been warned. Welcome."

As we filed out in silence from the hall my eye caught through an open door flasks, tripods, retorts, and three enormous models of molecules, which ones I couldn't tell. I slipped inside the science lab. It was rudimentary by American standards but the basic equipment was here, I could see that: for establishing the means to build and destroy. I was standing in front of the largest model seeing if I could fathom that molecular structure when my head was jerked backward.

I was staring up into the face of a priest.

"Who gave you permission to be in here?"

"No one, Father, I—"

"No one? And you a new boy too!"

With that Father Kieran hit me across the face so hard that I burst into tears. And once I started crying, I couldn't stop. Ten minutes later I was sitting in Grimshaw's office with a cup of warm tea in my hands, gazing at his unrelenting smile.

"So," he said, "you're interested in science, are you? A real chip off the old block. You've had a long journey, boy. And you'll be missing your mother, I suppose."

"No, sir."

■

I remember those winters. Parsippany had winters too. Sometimes cold, sometimes mild. Once we even wintered in Colorado, and I remember snow and ice and toboggans. But it had never occurred to me that anywhere in the world, even at the polar caps, could be as cold as Southwell in December. There was no hot water. There was supposed to be hot water, but it never worked. There was plenty of cold water, except when it got so cold the pipes froze. And that was the only time we ever counted our blessings, though we were exhorted to do so every day.

The window of my dormitory looked out onto the moorside. And in the odd moments left me between study, prayers, and being shouted at, I would stare out over that great crouching presence. It changed color with the seasons. Green, red, ocher, and gray. Gray when the lashings of snow came down, driven on by fierce northeasterlies. Great explosions of snow mixed in with the darkness. I came to love that moor, except when I was made to run up it. By Father Kieran, the games master.

Most of these teachers were priests, you must understand. And their celibacy was sometimes a little unresolved. One of the texts they taught us was Saint Paul's: It is better to marry than to burn. But they burned. Not all with the same bright flame, but they burned all right. Southwell's poem "The Burning Babe" was carved on a wooden panel in the Hall. Some of them hit us in a casual routine of greeting, in corridors, in classrooms, even at mass. I think it may have been the only physical contact they could comfortably make. After a while you no longer resented it: these were the conditions of life. The odd clout from them was easier to put up with than my mother had been. And here at least I had some allies.

Dr. Grimshaw was not a priest. He had taken on the job at short notice during the war, on the death of Monsignor Gillespie. And now, to the obvious irritation of Kieran and others, he was still there. He seemed to hate some of the priests around him, the ones for whom their religion had become nothing but a job. He also loathed the corporal punishment which seemed no more than an extension of their bodies, what their hands did when otherwise unoccupied. I liked Grimshaw. He was, I suspected, a little mad—and that made him interesting and alarming by turns. And made his world coherent too, for however mad he was, he had been made that way by lukewarm minds accepting contradiction; minds that didn't need, as he often put it, to get to the bottom of things. What he knew burned him. I think this was the reason that the only subjects I was any good at were the ones he taught—science, art, and religion. An odd combination—the men who should be teaching you these subjects properly, he told us, went to the war and never came back. I'm an odd-job man, boys, no more—for that's the way the Lord's appointed it. I'm learning as I go along, as you are yourselves.

My taste for science I've come to think was inherited anyway. Maybe the religion too, though Grimshaw made it into a logical study of great precision and beauty. He would never teach anything but the penny catechism. It's all you'll ever need, he'd say. Far more than you'll ever need, if the truth be known. Most people fill up their heads with acres of rusting machinery that never worked properly in the first place and is now completely defunct. Can't plow a field, can't knit a sweater. Learn what is in this little book, boys, he told us, and the age's fatuity need never ensnare you. The purpose of art was as simple. You'll never see, he said, unless you learn to draw. And unless you see, you'll never know who's out to cheat you.

This was my real education. Anything else I learned was only to avoid a beating. In which endeavor, I frequently failed.

The memories have coalesced and intermingled and I can no longer be sure of their sequence. I see him up front there with the little red book in his hand; or drawing atomic structures on a blackboard; or leaning over my sketch with loving irritation saying, "Clarity of outline, boy. Never mind the smudges in the middle. Find the form. Try to get that sludge out of your mind, out of your eye."

Without much thinking about it, I'd assumed I was going home to Parsippany for Christmas. Then Grimshaw brought me into his office and read out the telegram from my mother:

> *Your stepfather and I have decided to take the honeymoon we never really had—at Niagara Falls. Exciting Tommy! Give you time anyway to settle with your new friends. You know how much we love you! Your Mummy and your (brand new) Daddy!*

"Uses a lot of exclamation marks, your mother," Grimshaw said sourly. "I certainly hope you don't think *you* should. It is an atrocious stylistic device when repeated. Exclamatio. Ecphonesis. Only ever use it rarely, boy. Even Shakespeare sometimes overdid it, though perhaps the texts. . . . Anyway, not to worry. Spend Christmas here with us. Myself and my sister. Give us a chance to get to know one another."

I realized, as I walked down the corridor from his room, that I wasn't too worried anyhow. Mr. Terry Quinn had entered the area I might once have occupied, but he was welcome to it. My mother dreamwalked her way through the first eleven years of my life. Half the time I spoke to her she appeared to be staring vacantly at someone who wasn't there. "It's the grief," they'd all said. But eleven years is a long time for such consistent grieving, and her sorrow always seemed to me to be aimed at herself. Hard for anyone else to gain an entry there at all. Some women simply have a genius for marrying vacancy and melodrama.

The day before the end of term I had my second confrontation with Kieran. He was whipping us toward the moorside on a sleety afternoon when I decided I'd had enough. I felt as though my lungs were turning inside out and heading for my throat. I dropped back to the end of the runners—not that I had far to go—then hopped it over the lowest bit of drystone walling I could see. The herd continued up the hill with Kieran barking. I waited till they were over the top and walked back down to the school. I got changed and drifted quietly into the Library. The corner where the art books were held was my favorite spot in the school, apart from bed.

There was something wrong with Kieran's eyes. It wasn't a squint—in fact a squint might have expressed the contrariness, the asymmetry of forces contending inside him, and made his presence easier to bear. His eyes could never rest on anything, they hunted constantly from one feature to another. This gave him a curiously animal demeanor. He had tracked me to the Library and stood over me now, twitching with menace in his running togs.

"You little bastard, Lynch! What right do you think you have sneaking off here while the others have to hack it over the moor? Well?"

I suppose it's odd but I wasn't scared of Kieran as he stood there hunching himself up for a slap. I knew he could hurt me but I didn't care. The hurt he could inflict didn't seem to matter.

"I come in here, Father," I said, "because by the time I've finished I've learned something. After I've run over the moor all I've learned is how cold it is up there—and I already know that."

The hand swooped down and grabbed me by the back of my neck. Off we went along the corridor, then clattering down the steps, where my knee hit a step that took the skin off. By the time we'd arrived at Grimshaw's office I was fighting for breath. Kieran gave a perfunctory knock at the door and dragged me in.

"Dr. Grimshaw, this little Yankee . . ."

Grimshaw was already across the table and unhanding me from Kieran's embrace.

"This little Yankee's bleeding, Father Kieran."

Kieran looked down with undisguised irritation.

"He probably did it escaping from the run," he said. "Jumping over the wall so he could sneak back here."

"No, I didn't, Father. I did it when you pulled me down the stairs by my neck."

Grimshaw pushed Kieran gently to the door and opened it.

"Father Kieran, one day you really must try reasoning with the boys instead of continually assaulting them. Reason's spoken of very highly by Saint Thomas Aquinas, you know. And you mustn't assume that nonviolence is merely a form of Asiatic impertinence. After all, Saint Francis, not to mention our Redeemer himself . . . but then you have pastoral duties to attend to, eh, Father? There are doubtless boys waiting out on the moors, I shouldn't wonder, about to freeze and whatnot. Off you go then, that's a good fellow."

He closed the door and turned to me with a smile.

"Bloody priests," he said quietly, and proceeded to bandage me up himself. "They made Thomas More cross too, you know. But always remember, Southwell was a priest. Don't judge them all by our beloved Father Kieran."

If anyone had driven Grimshaw's car around in Parsippany, small crowds would have gathered on the sidewalks to examine it. I'd never seen a vehicle so small. It was an Austin Seven and it felt pretty crowded with the two of us in it, though he said it was what the British thought of as a sensible family sedan. But when I saw the size of the roads it had to drive along I understood its modest dimensions.

"I've saved up years of petrol coupons for you, my boy," Grimshaw said cheerfully as we drove out one day. "There are things you must see, things your father would have wished you to see. Look at Yorkshire closely enough, you'll understand the world."

So the vacations began with Grimshaw driving me from one location to another through the dales, talking incessantly. No one has ever spoken to me like that before or since. It was as though he had been preparing all his life to tell me these things and now had to get them off his chest without a pause. Most of it I didn't understand, but that didn't seem to trouble him.

"You will," he said, staring at me with those unnerving, fixed eyes I was growing used to.

Numerous times he shook me awake as I dozed off in the passenger seat.

"Wake up, boy. There'll be a time for sleeping. This is the time for listening. Learning. Making sense of the past before it swallows you whole. They own the past, you understand. You're trespassing on their land. They bought it."

We were standing in the ruined chapter house of Jervaulx Abbey.

"Can you read, Thomas Lynch?" Grimshaw was asking as he walked from one standing column to the next.

"Yes, sir."

"Read this, then. Read it to me."

He gestured to a fragment of masonry at his feet.

"I . . . I don't understand, sir."

He took my hand and placed it on the chamfered edge of one of the freestanding columns.

"Know what you're touching, do you? Four hundred years of lies, that's what, and four hundred years of truth. Four hundred years on either side of its destruction."

He let go of my hand and started to tap his head against the stone of the column, gently at first but then harder until with his last blow he made a large enough graze to show red.

"You've hurt yourself, sir."

"Good. That's where understanding starts . . . with a little pain. I'm going to show you how to read, young Lynch, and don't you ever forget what I say to you. It doesn't matter how much of it you understand. Just make sure you don't forget it.

"We should be grateful for these stones here, do you know why, Tom? Simply because they left them here for us at all. Their sons called out for bread and they gave them stones, but we should be grateful for that. Arthington and Baysdale, Beverly and Cottingham, North Ferriby and Nun Appleton—there's no remains at all. No stones, you see. Only stories. And the stories which the king tells do tend to prevail.

"You're looking at a diary entry in the pages of English history. The date is 1537. Abbot Sedbergh, who presided over this place of prayer, is scratching his own name in stone in the Tower of London. In a few weeks he'll be put to death at Tyburn. Two years earlier they'd killed off Thomas More. Dean Swift, who had no particular love of papists, called Thomas the most virtuous man these islands ever produced—and you are named after him. Did you know that?"

I didn't.

"The Pilgrimage of Grace has already been betrayed. Now the king's commissioners set to work. You can almost hear those larrikins come whistling down the lane, can't you? Let's pray to God you and I never have to meet them. Anyway, they move in and the monks move out, to wander the roads begging for alms. They stripped its treasures, which were considerable, to line their own pockets and those of the conniving local gentry. Gentlefolk indeed, and some of them still here. Then they blew it up. What were they so frightened of, that they had to do that? You're standing in your church here, Master Lynch, and it's had its roof blown off. The church of the four winds.

"All you'll ever be given either to understand or worship is ruins. Anything you ever come to understand about yourself will be through reading ruins."

It was a cold and windy day and Grimshaw came over to me rubbing his hands. His face had such a look of bewildered intensity that I wondered for a moment if he might be about to hit me.

"And all you'll ever glean of your own father's death will be from ruins too. That's all that's left now of his truth. Always make sure you know who's interpreting the wreckage, lad. Everyone's got a tale to tell in this life."

We crisscrossed the county in that little car. We had the roads largely to ourselves as Grimshaw burned away his hoarded petrol rations. He talked as though no one had ever listened before. Sometimes I came to wonder if what the boys said about him back at the school might not be true: that he was not, as I had supposed, a little mad, but entirely so.

"The terrain never stops shifting, take a note of that. I mean cast your eye back far enough through millennia, and Airedale over the hill there's a great shifting mountainous valley of ice with muck on its back. This county's riddled with the Reformation's ruins. Fountains and Easby, Bolton and Lastingham, Jervaulx and Whitby, Roche, Sawley, Kirkstall. All around the devastation's perpetrated. Those stones are signatures and I for one still recognize the names on them. I memorized the register. Elizabethan settlement! Elizabethan tyranny! They've taught us to be polite about it.

"This place never made peace easily with its oppressors. The Brigantes (their beehive querns tomorrow, bring your book) fought like demons for their Celtic independence. The Roman administrators of imperium. Came here to classify and rule. Someone must, I suppose, but we don't take kindly to it.

"As with state, so with Church. When the Church gets incorporated she becomes pliant. Lifts her skirts up when she should say no. Like that Concordat in 1933—with Nazis, no less. If the Church in Germany hadn't had too much to lose, that Concordat would never have been signed. Perhaps we'd come to love the world, couldn't bear to be separated from it.

"All the same, it could be worse, I daresay. Without that Concordat you'd not be here with me now."

Grimshaw had almost driven me to sleep with his dronings but I registered this.

"How's that, sir?" I said.

"Oh, my boy, your life must explain that to you, for I can't. You must pray for enlightenment. It's the only way, you know. A very good place to pray, Tom, should you be so inclined, is the apse at the end of the college chapel. All the images there are of Christ's scourging. Most unusual. In fact, I believe, unprecedented. The architect, Joseph Canning, thought that apse was inescapable; that we were all being scourged there daily. His wife died of cancer, you know—but it took ten years. And by the end she was all skin and bone. Skin and bone and agony. All night they could hear her cries from the bottom of the street. That apse—it's a kind of shrine, I suppose, to Mrs. Canning's pain. And it's always struck me as an appropriate place to pray."

We were approaching Scarborough from Seamer and Grimshaw suddenly darkened again.

"We're following in Leland's footsteps, would you believe it, that wretched sycophant. He came this way, notching up the priories and abbeys that his monarch was destroying—and making bloody sure he got his hands on plenty of loot for his own library. Filthy man."

He fell silent then and drove with unusual concentration until we came to the seafront. He stopped the car by the edge of the harbor and got out, beckoning me to follow. As we walked along the harbor wall his mood lightened. He started quoting in a singsong voice:

"This precious stone set in the silver sea,
Which serves it in the office of a wall,
Or as a moat defensive to a house,
Against the envy of less happier lands . . .

"Ever read Shakespeare, Tom?"

"They read some bits out at school, sir."

"Ah, yes, I suppose they do. But you must pay him more attention than that, you know, you really must, if you're ever to fulfill the potential your father's early departure left so . . . unfulfilled."

He was staring out over the North Sea as the waves crashed on the stone beneath us. He talked almost to himself, his eyes fixed on the horizon where a solitary freighter was steaming southward.

"I wrote a book on Shakespeare, Tom, not that they'd publish it. I must have been mad ever to have submitted it. Didn't want anyone stating the obvious after all these years. It started very simply by asking why the third line of the first play we think Shakespeare ever wrote, *The Comedy of Errors,* talks of a merchant of Syracusa—hardly an everyday phrase then any more than now. My explanation was simple enough—because those words provide an anagram of the word recusant. And because merchant was the code name used by Catholic mission priests in Elizabethan England. It's noticeable too that when Shakespeare described

. . . the melancholy vale,
The place of death and sorry execution
Beside the ditches of the abbey here

that when he describes, Tom, the execution that didn't take place in his play, he is also describing one that did. Because in 1588, one year before that play was performed, opposite Burbage's Theatre in Shoreditch stood Holywell Priory, the convent of nuns they closed down in 1539. And that's where they butchered William Hartley. And Shakespeare saw it because he was staying in that theater at that time. It haunted his mind and it haunts his little comedy.

"Now once the mind starts to move along these tracks, Tom, it's hard to slow it down again, you know. The Spiritual Testament of John Shakespeare proved beyond doubt that Shakespeare's father was a recusant. But Victorian Protestants didn't know what to do with this, any more than they knew what to do with the extravagant honesty of Thomas More—except ignore it, or pretend that it was otherwise.

"John Oldcastle, you see, was one of Foxe's founding martyrs and Shakespeare went and turned him into Falstaff. What he'd done there was to commit the unpardonable sin of telling a little truth in place of hagiography. So irritated were the functionaries of the time that the government spy, Anthony Munday, had to counterblast the following year with another play which presented the sanctified old rogue as being traduced by malignant priests and nuns. A lot of old tosh, frankly. The tradition's divided the wheat from the chaff there at least. . . . And Oldcastle died a Catholic, by the way, not that anyone's interested.

"Then I started to think about *Hamlet*. I started to think about the obvious things, things far too obvious for an Arden editor to mention. 'Get thee to a nunnery,' Hamlet shouts in 1601. A little odd that, you know. All the nunneries had been looted, sacked, and demolished sixty years before. You might think its resonance with an audience of the time deserved at least a footnote, eh, Tom?

"In that play Hamlet's holy mother gives herself up to a new master who is adulterous, gluttonous, and sacrilegious—and who has killed off a far holier father. I don't think the crowd in 1601 would have needed any footnotes or prompts to be reminded of the last king but one. . . . Anyway.

"Look at *Measure for Measure*, for goodness' sake. The ceremonies of confession and absolution are endorsed as routes to truth and reconciliation. And what is this force but the power of truth moving in disguise in a monk's habit through the troubled, misruled kingdom? Hearing confessions and shriving? This agent of atonement that must hide from the authorities. And Isabella kept from her convent, from her chastity, her silence, by the need to fight injustice in the civil realm. They call it a problem play. Stuff and bloody nonsense. It wouldn't be a problem play if they *read* it.

"Shakespeare smelt the stink of the times, he saw the filth of the times, he heard the obscenity of the times but he did not *succumb* to them. The actor Beeston—a Catholic, mind you—said of him: 'He lived in Shoreditch and was the more to be admired because he was *not* a company-keeper, and would not be debauched.' And old Archdeacon Davies said, 'He died a papist.' But they don't want to know. And, that's why, my young friend, my book remains unpublished."

Grimshaw looked down at me for the first time. I was shaking with cold but had learned never to interrupt his monologues.

"Well?" he said.

"What's recusant?" I asked, having kept the word carefully inside my head.

"Good," he said, "that's very good. When you don't understand, ask and keep asking until you're happy with the answer. Fish and chips we'll have and I'll explain it to you."

It was already growing dark by the time we came back to town, but he insisted on stopping the car down by Briery Wood Farm. We stumbled up onto the edge of the moor until we arrived at the rock. I could only just make out the markings in the bad light.

"Know what that shape is, boy?"

It was the first time that day I'd been able to answer one of his questions. I brightened in the gloom. "Yes, sir. It's a swastika."

"And how did you recognize the shape?"

"It was Hitler's shape, sir, he had it on his flags."

"Well, Hitler didn't put this one here. It was carved on this stone thousands of years ago by people who worshiped fire. They worshiped the light at least, not darkness. There are only three left in the whole world. Fifteen years ago your father and I stood here just like this as the light died. The day the Vatican signed its Concordat with Herr Hitler's government.

"Swastika's a Sanskrit word that means well-being and good fortune. And the stones of truth, remember, are precisely the ones employed to build the temple of defilement.

"Come on, boy. You've seen enough for one day. Agatha will have the meal ready."

As we drove the short distance down to his house near the river, I asked with my newfound confidence, "What is the time of reversal, sir?"

He turned and looked at me with affectionate surprise.

"Where did you come across that phrase?"

"It was a letter my father wrote to my mother—I found it in one of her drawers. . . . I suppose I shouldn't have, really."

"Take whatever information you can find," he said, "there's little enough forthcoming. Now, let's see, where do we start here?

"One night last century Pope Leo XIII had a dream, a dream of such extraordinary vividness that he believed it to be a vision. And in his vision he was told that this century we've landed in was to be given to Satan. That these were the last days. Now the last days are the time of reversal, when bad is called good, when serpents will speak in the name of the Lord and people will believe them. You must look at everything carefully, Tom, for nothing is necessarily what it seems.

"'Children, it is the last hour; and as you have heard that antichrist is coming, so now many antichrists have come; therefore we know that it is the last hour . . .' That's the apostle John. And, now we're home. To a nice hot fire and some dumplings."

Grimshaw's sister watched me attentively. Her skin seemed to be wrapped around her bones, with no flesh beneath it to soften the angle of her features. Her gray hair was pulled so tightly off her face I thought her scalp might split off from her forehead.

"I hope you haven't exhausted the boy, Patrick, you do go on so relentlessly. You've grazed your head again. Must you be so theatrical?"

"There's my reputation to consider," he said evenly. "Don't worry about the boy. He has enough of his father in him to cope with my relentlessness. Feed him."

The dumplings came. I was halfway through my second plate when she spoke, though I knew she had been watching me carefully from the other side of the table. Without looking up, I'd felt that gaze.

"How's your mother, Thomas? Still wrapped up in herself?"

I'd never heard my mother described like that before but it didn't seem a bad way of putting it.

"Yes," I said, "mutters to herself, makes strange faces. Or did before . . ."

"I remember. The first time your father ever brought her here we said afterward, 'Well, opposites attract, obviously.'"

"My mother and father came *here*?" I asked, as my mouth fell open.

"My dear boy, your mother and father *lived* here till poor Tom's, well, until your father. . . . Close your mouth, boy, there's half-chewed food in it. Now that I do find truly repulsive.

"Patrick, what exactly have you been lecturing the boy about? The second coming, I suppose, just as you did with his father. Can't you feed him at least a few crumbs about his own life?"

"I have attempted to indicate the nature of the times, Agatha, no more," Grimshaw said, staring out of the window at the river. "Darker in the belly of the beast than it is out there."

"We'd best eat our trifle quickly, then," she said, and went out to get it.

❷

Delaquay

It was Baudelaire in The Painter of Modern Life *who pointed out that none of the drawings of Guys was signed. If by a signature one understood merely those forgeable characters that spell a name.*

A L F R E D   D E L A Q U A Y ,   *Diaries*

SO THE GRIMSHAWS' HOME BECAME MY HOME AND WHEN I WASN'T at school I was there.

"What sort of house is this exactly, sir?" I once asked Grimshaw.

"Nondescript Wharfedale vernacular," he said. "Solid, mind you. Good millstone grit. When half of New York City has fallen into the Hudson, this will still be standing. Another reason for you to stay, Tom."

Not that I had much choice in the matter. My mother sent a present at Christmas and another on my birthday. That was it.

"Don't worry," Agatha said, "she wouldn't have anything intelligent to say to you even if you were there. She'd just hum and frown and look in the mirror."

Things improved in time. For one thing Kieran stopped hitting me when he realized I'd become the Head's adopted son. And rationing ceased, finally. Imperceptibly my accent changed so the other boys no longer shouted, "Yank," when they saw me on the street, though I'm told the way I speak is still strange. Neither one thing nor another, some say, an oddity regarding the provenance of my vowels. There was even a little romance, too, though not for long.

She was the daughter of the owner of the local fish shop and I was attracted I think by the sweet placidity of her demeanor. Also by the fact that she kept smiling at me, which was the first time any girl had done that. I invited her for tea at Agatha's prompting. She didn't say much during the two hours we were in the house, it was true. She giggled a lot, which I at least found winning.

"The child's dense," Agatha said, when I returned from walking her home. "Just like your mother. All soft looks and internal vacancy. Don't, for God's sake, make the same mistake your father made, boy. With a mind like his too, choosing that . . . that . . ." Agatha's voice petered out.

However nondescript the outside of the Grimshaws' house might have seemed to its neighbors in Yorkshire, the inside was astonishing. Half library and half gallery, most walls contained at least one of the mysterious and compelling images by Delaquay which brother and sister seemed to have obsessively collected. This was the one enterprise in which they were entirely united. From my first day in the house these images had captured me. Grimshaw saw me standing in front of one of them.

"Good boy," he said, "your eyes work as well as your brain. Know who he is?" he asked.

"No, sir."

"Read the signature, then."

I stared along the bottom edge of the picture as hard as I could.

"I can't see one, sir."

"That's because there isn't one," he said delightedly. "Delaquay never signed his works any more than the men who built the cathedrals did."

"How do you know they're his, then?"

"No one else ever drew quite like this. Also his missing signature became in the end . . . a kind of signature."

"Then wasn't it self-defeating, sir?"

"No, I don't think so. I think that just for once it was the world that suffered the defeat. He didn't need anything of the world, you see. He was independently wealthy. He made up his own rules for the Delaquay Society. We don't have this collection here because of our wealth, you know—we really have very little money. It's because of our devotion to his . . . cause."

It was while looking at those pictures of Delaquay, and at the strange little book about the artist which they gave me to read, that I started to see properly, just as old Grimshaw had predicted. All the other books about art in that house I read, if I can put it this way, in relation to the Delaquays. For these pictures were there, and they were real. They summoned me back daily with ever greater intensity. I, too, became obsessed.

There was in particular a tiny triptych which I stared at most of all. There were three faces and each one gazed out from behind a veil like the pictures of the face of Jesus imprinted on Veronica's napkin. One portrayed Christ in the tomb, between crucifixion and resurrection but filled somehow with life, true life, and spirit behind those closed eyes. The second showed the Magdalene, ravaged with her grief. The third was a face somewhere between jeering and self-torture, a terrible image of the self-consumption of hatred.

"There is a debate about this one, even in the Society itself," Grimshaw said. "Some say it's Judas halfway between the High Priest and Potter's Field. Some say it's Satan at the precise moment Christ descends to hell. If you take the Satanic interpretation, and this depends partly on how far down you think Delaquay himself descended, then this is the one true moment of sadness for the devil. Christ has entered his domain and brought the light of goodness there for the first and only time. Satan has taken what he had no right to touch. He has introduced into the darkness the light that has no place there and in that terrible blaze of truth he sees the ultimate destruction of his kingdom."

Grimshaw took this last one off the wall and handed it to me.

"Go and draw what you see in it," he said.

I spent the weekend doing copies, the last one I thought coming remarkably close to the texture of Delaquay himself. I even caught something of those strange imploding eyes. I took it down proudly to Grimshaw, who was reading by the window. He examined it for a moment without expression, then said, "It's clever, Tom, but only that. You've merely copied him."

"But you told me to copy him," I protested.

"No, I didn't. I told you to draw what you saw there. But you've only peeled the surface off with your eyes.

"We live in the order of signs. Delaquay knew that, at least. No one was a greater sacramentalist than he himself, whatever the Dark Theorists have to say about it. If you merely steal another man's sign instead of forging your own, that makes you a counterfeiter.

"I think you'll have to live with this picture for a while before you start to see it. Take it up to your room and keep it there."

So that was how I came to live for two years with an image at my bedside of Satan. Or was it Judas? Either way it made a pleasant enough change from the portrait of my mother it supplanted.

3

Hindenburg

People often spoke of them as birds, great birds in magisterial flight, but to me they were giant silver fishes, floating through the same invisible water that held the clouds.
ERNST WAIGEL, *Zeppelin*

GRIMSHAW DID NOT TAKE MANY CLASSES ANYMORE. YOUNGER men had filled the long-vacant positions. From time to time, though, he would descend from his eyrie in the north wing to give a half-hour lecture on whatever had been preoccupying him of late. These were much valued by the boys since no preparation was necessary, for no one ever had the foggiest notion what they would be about.

Even so, I was startled this particular day when he began to speak with his usual intensity.

"Today, boys, I'm going to talk to you about the crash of the *Hindenburg* dirigible in 1937. There is a certain poignancy in the subject since that terrible event removed Lynch's father from our lives.

"Tom Lynch Senior was in my opinion the finest alumnus of this school. I was proud to be his teacher and, later in life, happy to be his friend. It has been my privilege to oversee the education of his only son.

"But first a little background.

"The wish to fly does seem to be innate in man. You will all remember from your classical studies the story of Icarus. At its simplest that is the story of what happens to man himself when he does not obey his father. That is, of course, how history starts—not listening to your father. That, give or take a snake or two, is pretty much the story of the Garden of Eden.

"What's often forgotten is the background to the flight of Daedalus and Icarus. Minos was the king of Crete and had initially welcomed the famous craftsman to his shores. But then he discovered how Daedalus had helped Pasiphaë couple with Poseidon's bull. He had used his ingenuity and artifice to facilitate bestiality. And the monstrous was brought forth from the miscegenation of two realms.

"It was the skill of Daedalus too which constructed a labyrinth in which the truth might be concealed. It was an example of the temple of defilement—there have been all too many in history. The continent of Europe this century has been filled with them. The stones of some remain still to tell their dreadful truths. Better than words can, probably. Words flinch from such . . . enormity.

"What you must remember about the flight of Icarus and his father is that it constituted an escape—perhaps even from history. To wish to escape from history is not ignoble, though it is impossible in this life. And because impossible, therefore a sin—a species of fantasy transposed to the realm of orthopraxis. Consequently, an inappropriateness, an extremity of inappropriateness—which is not a bad definition of both sin and heresy. Their attempted escape ended, like so many, in disaster. And one can imagine how Daedalus felt when he lifted his only son waterlogged out of the waves to carry him off and bury him, a victim of his own ingenuity. Classical man is not so far from modern man here, you know. I can vouch for that.

"In fact the only means of escape from a Paris encircled and besieged during the Franco-Prussian War was by balloon. Such are the labyrinths men still make of their lives.

"And there was one fellow apparently who fastened eagles to a spherical container, but though the Lord gave us dominion over the fowls of the air, the birds wouldn't cooperate. His scheme never got off the ground.

"For two centuries men have been rising up into the air, and for thousands of years before that they dreamed about it. The Montgolfier Brothers were up there back in 1783, in a paper balloon inflated with hot air. You have to displace the air, you see, with something lighter, even if it's only the air itself heated up. But you must arrive at something which is lighter than its environment. And a thousand cubic feet of air weighs about eighty pounds. The same amount of hydrogen weighs less than six pounds. So why not fill your airship up with . . . hydrogen, for example? Can you think of a reason, Lynch, why one shouldn't do that?"

I looked up at Grimshaw, not sure what his game was.

"Well, it's highly flammable, sir," I said.

"It's highly flammable, yes. And not only that, but explosive if contaminated with six percent or more of air. Helium on the other hand is nonflammable, but the United States has a monopoly on its production from natural gas. This plays its part in our little story here because the *Hindenburg would* have been filled up with helium, except the Americans wouldn't let the Germans have any, for reasons both economic and political.

"History intrudes, you see, boys, even in a matter as apparently innocent as technology. When the zeppelin went down at Echterdingen, the crowds were singing 'Deutschland, Deutschland Über Alles'—and, believe me, whenever anyone wants to put a country above everything else, you can guarantee that before too long there'll be murder in the streets. The airships had become a nationalist symbol. Soon they were used for throwing bombs about in the Great War.

"Dr. Joseph Goebbels gave two million marks toward the construction of the *Hindenburg,* and Goebbels was not the Air Minister, remember—that was Hermann Göring. Goebbels was in charge of propaganda. The big gas bag spoke, you see. Up there in the air it spoke to the world and what it said was: German power. And German power meant Nazi power. It put the swastika into the heavens.

"What I'm trying to say to you, boys, is that you mustn't lament the *Hindenburg.* It was right that it should go up in flames. The only matter for grief is all those who died with it. This was Nazi Germany in miniature, floating from country to country. It was a hotel in the clouds. Why, they even had a special piano made out of aluminum so someone could tickle the ivories while they sipped dry martinis. They were more comfortable in that room above us than we are in this. Meanwhile, below on the ground—on the ground of their own country—the killing had started.

"Many men have come tumbling out of the sky with their craft in flames. In a sense that is the history of aviation. But some of these were not aviators. Their lives in that sense should not have been forfeit."

Grimshaw had grown distracted with the last words he had spoken. He turned and looked out through the window at the moors, where there was already some bad cloud gathering. When he spoke again, it was almost to himself.

"You must remember her ETA was 0600 hours. It was the head winds that delayed her for over twelve hours. No one could possibly have expected that at the time.

"There was something clumsy and helpless about it, hard to describe, nose down as though sniffing for a patch of safety. Then everything was alight, men falling through the air alight. And the screaming. At least the swastikas were burned to nothing. That was the one part of the holocaust we might still applaud."

The bell had rung a few moments before and as Grimshaw fell silent the boys started to slide from their seats a little uneasily and leave. I waited until the last of them had gone and walked over to him, still sitting there, staring out of the window.

"You were there, weren't you? Why didn't you tell me?"

Grimshaw turned his face toward me.

"You wouldn't have understood. Not then. Perhaps not even now. I went to meet Tom . . . your father. We had no conception . . . there were risks, obviously.

"After it, I had to continue. There was nothing else to do except continue. I went on to New York to the Delaquay Convention, the 1937 Convention. We were both of us expected, your father and myself. They had a minute's silence to honor him. Tonight, Tom, I'll give you your father's copy of the book. I'd meant to give it to you when you went up to Oxford next term. Now seems a better time. I will give you it by way of . . . apology."

That evening Grimshaw handed me the *Paradise Lost*. It was bound in heavily stained vellum and it was folio. A big, weighty volume. I opened it and read the colophon:

PRINTED AT THE BERMONDSEY PRESS
ON INDIA PAPER
FOR THE DELAQUAY SOCIETY
WITH ORIGINAL INK DRAWINGS
BY ALFRED DELAQUAY

THIS EDITION IS LIMITED TO ONE

1908

"Limited to one?"

"It was characteristic of Delaquay. It was part of his strategy."

"And the drawings?"

"Are the originals tipped in."

"But shouldn't it be reproduced? Shouldn't something like this be made available?"

"He believed not. Indeed he made sure there was not 'something like this.' Only this. He made them partly in protest at the depredations of lithography. That's what he said, anyway. And he made it a condition of their being passed on that the new possessor should agree never to allow one to be reproduced. He said he'd rather have them destroyed.

"So I must ask you, Tom, for that promise before you accept this book."

"Can't I at least look at it first?"

"No. Your father understood when I gave it to *him*."

"*You* gave this book to my father?"

"Of course. How else would he have come by it? It was I who proposed him for membership of the Delaquay Society, membership of which is a condition of being the holder of that book. Or any other."

"You mean I have to join the society before I can take the book?"

"Yes."

"But how do I join?"

"By accepting the book and the conditions accruing thereto."

"What are the conditions?"

"That the book can never be sold or traded but only exchanged for one of the other Delaquay Society editions. And that no part of it may be reproduced in any form other than those sanctioned by the Society in its own publications, which are not for sale, or distribution, to the public. It shouldn't even be seen except by another member."

"How would I know, then, if someone is a member?"

"Because he or she will have one of the editions."

"So you know how many editions there are?"

"We think we do, or at least we have a very good idea, but we can't be absolutely sure. Delaquay's life was a mysterious business, and it is possible he produced and distributed more books than we have cataloged. That possibility is always in our minds. Anyway, I must revert to my question. I speak now, you must understand, as a Society member, not an individual."

I was already turning the pages of this book, those extraordinary first pages. My life was already unraveling.

"I suppose I accept."

"Good. Fewer than fifty people have ever set eyes on that book, Tom. Your father would be pleased to know that you're one of them at last."

I took the book up to my room and started turning the pages.

I sometimes wonder if I've ever stopped.

What could be so special about an illustrated edition of *Paradise Lost*? After all, it's hardly unique. Blake did one, as did John Martin and Doré. It was not even a work for which I had any particular fondness.

Along with Johnson I could imagine no man wishing it longer. And yet . . .

There was something about the inside of that book which made it different from anything else I'd ever moved my eyes across. It wasn't merely knowing that these illustrations were the original drawings which had never, if Grimshaw were to be believed, been reproduced anywhere or at any time; or that so few hands and so few eyes had ever caressed it. There was something else as well. He had not merely illustrated the book, he had somehow in the process also illuminated the text. I understood now why it could only be an edition of one. The aura surrounding it would otherwise be dispelled. Because of the juxtaposition of word and image, he had made the text on the page unique too. I started to read and I realized that in some indefinable manner this was not the same work I'd slaved over at school. And then I saw that illustration.

The lines chosen were picked out in red by a change of rubric in the text itself:

Him the Almighty Power
Hurl'd headlong flaming from th'ethereal sky
With hideous ruin and combustion down . . .

I picked up the book and went down the stairs to Grimshaw, who was standing by the window staring out into the dark. I laid the book down on the table beside him, open at that page.

Grimshaw glanced down at it then turned back to the window.

"Yes, I know," he said. "Believe me, I've spent a great deal of my life looking at that picture."

"It's the *Hindenburg*," I said.

"Certainly very similar. And the creatures who come out flaming from that tear in its belly . . .

"These are grave matters, Tom. The whole point of Delaquay's existence was to (how shall I say it?) *italicize* their gravity. No graver, of course, than the words of Milton himself, and that's the point too. Now you have the book, you might start to understand. I'm not sure I ever have."

He turned and looked at me carefully, reading my expression.

"The British regarded the airships as a naval affair. This was on the perfectly logical basis that they were craft dependent on displacing the element in which they were entirely submerged. So their nearest parallel was evidently the submarine.

"I can't explain anything to you, Tom, you must understand that. Nor can anyone else. Beware anyone who comes to you with explanations.

"Many people through the years have thought that theirs was the last age. And logically speaking they must be wrong, of course—excepting only the once.

"Great fishes fly in the air and men fall out of their wombs in flames. They build squat stone temples for the slaughter of men, women, and children.

"Millions, Tom, not an occasional ritual outrage. A greater number than Jacob could have thought his seed would ever amount to . . . scientific temples of defilement. While away to the east a man rises up who calls himself the leader of nations. Who smiles quietly while destroying his own millions. Millions upon millions. If this isn't the last time then perhaps the Lord *has* abandoned us to our iniquity. Closed the book of mankind once and for all."

Grimshaw turned down the cover of *Paradise Lost*. He lifted the book up and handed it to me.

"Do you understand yet why there's only one copy of this?"

"Yes."

"Otherwise it would lose its meaning immediately. A meaning only just recovered. Precariously. Between these covers."

I nodded.

"You see how much work and devotion was necessary for him to stop the pages canceling the words."

I nodded again.

"There is a tradition in the Society that whichever edition of a book is held by a man at the time of his death, one of the illustrations will have prefigured it. It is one of the reasons the books can never be reproduced. It would be impossible to explain to people their . . . potency."

"The drawings I've been doing . . ."

"Your little copies, yes . . ."

"Don't they constitute some kind of reproduction?"

"No. Mechanical reproduction was what he wished to avoid. He told me that."

I thought for a moment.

"So then if someone could reproduce his work in its entirety by hand, he would not be condemned for doing so?"

Grimshaw looked a little uneasy.

"He said not. Delaquay said that such a copy would be permissible."

"But why?"

"Because he said the person who could reproduce him so personally and entirely would by necessity have had to endure the same truths that he did."

"And?"

"Would therefore have become indistinguishable from himself."

4

Catechism

Devil with devil damned
Firm concord holds, men only disagree
JOHN MILTON, *Paradise Lost*

IT WAS TO BE THE LAST CLASS I'D EVER HAVE WITH GRIMSHAW. For the other boys I think it was pure relief. My feelings were mixed to the point of confusion. Grimshaw meant more to me than just a teacher, but on the other hand he was never *less* than a teacher. I would miss him. Would I find another Grimshaw in Oxford?

He came in holding the little red catechism and as he held it up to the class the other boys groaned. He smiled at us all broadly.

"Ah, what grown-up young fellahs, eh? Too old for the catechism now, are we? Learned it all and passed on, no doubt. Ready to talk about existentialism and such-like matters. Well, this is going to be my last chance to say this to you, so I'm going to say it.

"If you could read this book once a week and think about it for one minute a week for the rest of your lives, it would be of more value to you—of *infinitely* more value to you—than ninety percent of what you will actually end up reading. However, for this last half hour before I relinquish you into the world, you can think about the teaching contained herein.

"I want to look at a couple of subjects raised in this little red book before you go off to your separate colleges and universities. The first one is how sinful it is to belong to a secret society, any sort of secret society that sets itself over against church or state. Saint Paul, you see, says how each soul should be subject to the higher power, for the one who resists that power resists God's providential scheme, and thereby obtains for himself damnation.

"That's the gist of the first point. And the second one's all about the fifth commandment. Now I'm sure you'll all remember what the fifth commandment is."

"Thou shalt not kill, sir."

"Thou shalt not kill. Exactly. Nor for that matter fill your heart with vengefulness and hate; nor put to death a man's good name with wounding words; nor even quarrel without the very best of reasons. It is, you see, the killing of any good and necessary thing between men that is at issue here.

"Now, gentlemen, I want you to think about something. I am not going to give you any answers for the very simple reason that I do not have any. And I think it perhaps appropriate that you leave this establishment remembering me as a fellow creature in perplexity. For I am one, you know.

"I would like you to think of 1933, before you were born, when the Vatican signed its Concordat with the newly established Nazi Government in Germany.

"A concordat, at the risk of sounding obvious, is that which implements, or endeavors to implement, concord. And concord represents a harmony of interests, a concurrence of desiderata. Now what harmony of interests could have existed between the Vatican hierarchy and Hitler's freshly born statal beast in 1933?

"Any ideas?"

Fairbrother raised a hand.

"Well?"

"The protection of Roman Catholics in the Reich, sir."

"Yes, good man. One can see, of course, why Rome should wish for that, but why should the National Socialists, I wonder, who in truth loathed all religions except their own murky and nihilistic one. The return of Baal, the sacrifice of children. What could have been their aim do you think, Fairbrother?"

"Keeping up appearances, sir?"

"Excellent. Precisely so. For they continued with their killing anyway. Hans and Sophie Scholl were butchered for their attempt to live the gospel. Gerlich, the editor of *Gerade Weg,* was very slowly beaten to death. Father Paul Metzger was hanged. It took four years before the Pope finally issued *Mit Brennender Sorge . . .* Fairbrother?"

"With burning concern, sir."

"Good. Four years. It wasn't until March of 1937 that the document of protest was released. And by then . . . the beast had developed an appetite, there in the labyrinth of the Reichstag building. Moral, Fairbrother?"

"Careful in picking your friends, sir?"

"Not bad. Take care defining your interest, too, lest in your gesture of self-defense you seal yourself into a tomb.

"Now how define your own interests? That in a way is what the whole of this little red book is about. And the crux of the matter is summed up when Jesus says, 'He who wishes to gain his life, must lose it for my sake.'

"Let's look at Saint Thomas More in 1530. Four hundred and three years before the Nazis started squirming with excitement on having a country—a whole country, perhaps even a whole century—to breathe their smoke across. Easy enough to define *his* interest, one would have thought. Recently made Chancellor of all England. He is the king's friend. His house in Chelsea boasts a magnificent library. Great artists like Holbein and humanist scholars like Erasmus come and stay with him. His interest in one sense of the word is to hang on to all this. At any cost, surely.

"He didn't, though. And because he didn't we call him saint rather than merely sir. He gave it all up, even his head, because he wouldn't lie. Would not bear false witness, you see. While another beast was beginning to itch with absolute power, with its acts of supremacy and submission of clergy, he relinquished all rather than turn his back on the truth of God.

"Now, who's the logician? Peters, you're the one going off to study philosophy, put the statements I've made together in that large, retentive mind of yours and tell me if you can sense any logical tension."

Peters pondered for a moment. Then this:

"The statement of Saint Paul could be used logically against Saint Thomas."

"Excellent. You have summed up the situation precisely. If we are to be exhorted to obey the authority above us, then this assumes that such an authority is always valid. In an instance where that is not the case, how are we to behave with propriety? How should we proceed against regimes which are . . . monstrous, and have therefore forfeited any authority over us? Must we fight them then, even without the express encouragement of the leaders of our own Church? And if we do fight, with what do we fight? Our own lives merely, or those of others too? Sometimes the lives of others might be implicated whether we choose it or not. . . .

"We have five minutes to go, then most of you will probably never hear my monotonous drone again. I would like you to indulge me in these final moments by considering the dilemma of Hamlet. Yes, I know you're groaning under your breath, but for the last time you'll have to listen to the old man's obsession with Shakespeare.

"He is a young man who is to inherit the highest position in the land. Fathered, remember, by a midnight ghost, and foster-fathered now by an incestuous impostor. And mothered by one who's so forgetful that she takes her husband's murderer between her legs at night and bids her son respect and love him.

"His interrupted studies, his new learning—all that's elsewhere. Here is lies, deceit, corruption. You can hear the truth if you choose— but only from the dead. That involves giving up your bed and allowing your wits to come astray. At least as this world construes such things.

"To be honest here, Hamlet begins to understand, is to be separated from the present. From the present moment and the present regime. A separation, if necessary, unto death. There are two women here. One betrays the memory of his father with the man who made his father a memory. The other lies because her father bids her lie. Because his lies are his authority, and she obeys the authority set over her, which costs her, in a different way, her life too.

"What has been banished from memory's kingdom returns to demand its vengeance. For here health itself, *sanitas,* has been defined as forgetting. This solitary figure draped in black calls their crimes to mind—so he must be defined as unhealthy, insane. Otherwise he threatens their survival. An antic disposition? This is mere hyperbole, a trope. It is a stance, no more, designed to disrupt the continuum of forgetfulness, to mark the time.

"He grows lyrical over a skull in a graveyard. Between childhood and death lie irony, separation, betrayal, more deaths. One jester long dead disinterred by another jester, while the prince they say is a lunatic looks on. And that's the second time in the play that the earth has opened to reveal a loved one changed for the worse.

"You see, this prince could only be enthroned by not being this prince at all. Only by stepping out of his space into theirs. Out of the air . . . But his logic is foreign to theirs, for his memory's not soluble in custom.

"Some critics have made a great song and dance about sexual repugnance in the play. They miss the point. *Everything* stinks. His father's death. His mother's passion. His stepfather's drinking and lust. Ophelia's duplicity, Yorick's remains, Rosencrantz and Guildenstern's craving to please. Polonius's body. It all stinks and it's all part of the stink that is the forgetfulness, the wicked oblivion that constitutes Denmark.

"How could he be joined to another amidst such decomposition? The warm flesh has already gone cold but carries on walking. It is the dead member that stands upright. His madness is at least a species of austerity. It is, quite properly, uncomforted.

"He tells his truth, this prince, though they beg him not to. And both Thomas More's wife and his beloved daughter Margaret begged him to conform; to come home to his blazing fire, leave the rats in the tower behind him. At the end of the play the stage is strewn with corpses, including his own. All this to tell a truth. Lies surely would be much cheaper, particularly when the state itself has swallowed them?

"Remember now as you make your way in life, boys: the king still carouses in his castle and he will till time ends. You can still see his torchlights there up on the hill if you keep your eyes open. Switch on the radio, you'll hear his voice. It's still commanding, still offering appointments. We all live in Denmark."

The bell was ringing. Grimshaw bowed to us all and left.

That last summer before Oxford was sheer delight. Grimshaw lent me the old Austin Seven and I drove back and forth across the dales, even spending the odd night in a boardinghouse in Scarborough. I would sit on the harbor wall drawing the fishing fleet and remembering that first trip here, the beginning of my life in England, my life with him and his sister.

Then it was time to go to university. To his profound irritation, I had accepted a place at the Isaac Lenau Institute of Fine Arts.

"But it's not even a college," he'd said. "What's the point in going to Oxford and not being part of a college?"

"I'll be affiliated to one."

"A different one each year."

"More variety for me then."

"Do leave the child alone, Patrick," Agatha said. "He's made his decision. It's his life."

"Anyway, you have your letter for Blanchard," he said. "He'll meet you at the station and take you to your rooms."

"My lodgings?"

"No, they are not lodgings, they are *rooms*. And it is part of the Society's bequest that they will be paid for in their entirety for the duration of your stay at Oxford. An account has been opened at Oxford and sufficient funds will also be deposited there—far too much, if you ask me—to meet all your requirements. You're welcome to come back here anytime you like, at Christmas, for example. But that's up to you. Unlike most students there, you'll have accommodation all year round. Make you the object of much envy, I should think, and . . . curiosity. So beware."

"Blanchard?"

"To be trusted, I suppose, insofar as it's ever possible to know such things."

"He is a member of the Society?"

"He holds the Blake. Quite beautiful. I've seen it three times. He's looking forward to seeing the Milton again. He also holds the Transactions of the Society. His is the most extensive library, in this country, anyway. So don't waste all your waking hours in that city chasing women."

"Patrick, please," Agatha said.

"Well, dear sister, men do, you know. Otherwise the race would doubtless perish. He only had one female companion here. That was for three hours and then you drove her away."

"She was so like—" She stopped herself.

"Even so. We're here if you need us, Tom. But you are in no way . . . obligated."

Agatha leaned across awkwardly and kissed me and I had a feeling she might be about to cry, a thing I'd never seen her do. But there was no time left to find out for the train was about to leave.

As I leaned from the window, staring at the two of them wrapped up against the autumn winds, a thought suddenly occurred to me.

"Did Blanchard know my father?" I asked.

"You'd best ask him."

I sank into the seat as the train chugged out of Bradford. My hand slipped into my pocket and fingered something which had not been there before. I pulled it out. It was his copy of the penny catechism—old and dog-eared, the one he'd always used and brandished at us. I opened the cover. Inside in Grimshaw's immaculate and tiny hand was written

Don't forget these rules, boy—even when your life dictates that you must disobey them.

5

Oxford

" . . . these college quadrangles! So gnawed by time as they are,
so blackened and so gray when they are not black."
NATHANIEL HAWTHORNE, *Notebooks*

OXFORD, 1956, AND THE THING TO REMEMBER IS THAT IT WAS ALL
in black and white. Hard to explain this without taking you back there.
The following year the Historic Buildings Fund would start its work,
scraping and scratching away the sooty skin so that underneath might be
revealed the honey of Cotswold stone, or the paler smoothness of Port-
land. But for now these walls are smudged with years of filth, an invisible
locust-covering of chemical deposits. Some of the colleges had faced
themselves with Virginia creeper or Roman cement to stabilize dilapida-
tion but decaying masonry was everywhere. Above the Bodleian the pin-
nacles rotted and no freshly chiseled Clipsham stone had yet come to
replace them. As for the Sheldonian emperors, those great weathered
slabs of heads stared blindly northward out of Oxford like the mis-
placed parts of Ozymandias.

It didn't bother me. I was fresh from Yorkshire and Yorkshire's in
black and white at least half the year. It's true there are great commo-
tions between moors, dales, and sky when spring finally gets started, but
whenever the weather has a point to make, everything's printed in black
and white again. Those photographs Bill Brandt took in the thirties
don't lie. The coal sheen that gets burned out in shrieks of white nothing-
at-all may be melodramatic. The white flesh round a miner's eyes against
the pitch of his face is melodramatic too. But then there are truths in

melodrama. The industry of the north was founded on a chiaroscuro—
moral as well as physical.

Blanchard met me at the station. The rain poured but Blanchard was
smiling. Bill Blanchard was always smiling. I think the muscles in his face
were that way inclined. He was six feet tall with jet-black hair creamed
back from his forehead. He wore a white trench coat that nearly came
down to his feet and he stood four-square beneath a vast umbrella.

"Thomas Lynch." He beamed. "Tom Tomasovich." At forty-one he
was exactly the age my father would have been had he lived. He took my
case from me.

"A drink, Tom. I've been waiting for half an hour and I am *bloody*
cold. You do drink?"

I nodded, never having considered the subject. Did I drink?
Grimshaw had occasionally given me a sherry, even two at Christmas,
and I had occasionally taken a half-pint with him in a moorside pub, so I
supposed I drank. I'd never made any effort not to.

Blanchard pressed the umbrella into my hand and set off swinging
my case to the nearest pub. Once inside the door, he shook his collar and
flapped his arms like a huge thin bird drying itself.

"Bitter?" he said, not waiting for a reply. "Two pints of bitter, then,
Jim."

We sat in a corner by the fire. He drank quickly so I did too. Within
ten minutes his glass was empty.

"Your round." He smiled. I bought two more pints.

"Why the Isaac Lenau Institute?" he asked. "Not one of Grimshaw's recommendations, surely."

"No, he tried to talk me out of it."

"Then why?"

"To study art," I said.

"You didn't have to do it there, old chap. Half of them can't even
speak English. Some of them are positively . . . well, let's say a little

unbalanced by their wanderings. You can actually get a respectable degree from the place, I trust?"

"Yes, they are affiliated for . . . all that."

Words like matriculation, graduation, honors were still lodged in my mind somewhere from the prospectus I had read, but they seemed a little long by now. I'd only eaten sandwiches in the last six hours and I'd never drunk as much as this before. A sudden rush of exhilaration had me beaming back at Bill as he beamed at me.

"You knew my father?" I asked.

"My best friend. Tipple Tom and Boozy Blanchard. Tom and Bill, the nightjars. Drunk everywhere in Oxford with your old man. Why, we've even drunk here in this very pub. Me in this chair and him in yours. A chip off the old block, I see, the way you're shifting those pints."

That night I slept in the bed I was to occupy for my years at the Lenau. I woke in the morning to my new life. Books—I'd never seen so many books before except in a library. They were behind glass in polished wooden cases all round the room. At the end from where I was lying, a staircase led to a little gallery which was also fitted with bookcases. In the middle of this was a door, which opened now as Bill came through in his dressing gown, carrying two cups of coffee. He sat down next to me and smiled. Reaching a hand into his pocket he took out his cigarettes and lit one.

"Do you smoke?" he said.

"No."

"Are you going to?"

"I hadn't really thought about it."

"I should," he said. "Whatever you don't make a conscious effort *not* to do, you'll end up doing. There speaks a philosophy tutor."

"Is that what you do?"

"I do a lot of things. Some tutoring, yes. I also receive a stipend from the Delaquay Society in New York for keeping the archive here. I write books no one wants to publish. I suppose I have that much in

common with old Grimshaw anyway. You have, I take it, been the bene-
ficiary of his views on Shakespeare?"

I nodded.

"Grimshaw's convinced they wouldn't publish his book because of
a Protestant conspiracy in Grub Street. In fact they wouldn't publish it
because . . . it's not very good, frankly. A few local insights but he never
gets past Bawden. You've read Bawden, of course?"

I shook my head.

"*The Religion of Shakespeare* by Henry Sebastian Bawden, of the
Oratory. 1899. It's over there in the corner case with all the other works
on Catholicism in England. You actually practice, do you?"

I nodded.

"I didn't know. What with Grimshaw."

Blanchard stopped suddenly and looked uneasy.

"Forgive me," he said, "I'm being impertinent. Blackfriars is five
minutes up the road. It's a pleasantly simple chapel. None of the frip-
peries and polychrome diversions that do seem to clutter some of the
churches. The plainchant's good, I believe."

He stood up and took my empty cup from me. He gestured with
his head toward a door behind me. "There's a kitchen down there we
share, though you won't see me in it much. There's food, drink, all you
need."

He put his hand into the pocket of his dressing gown and took out
a key.

"This is yours. You must come and go as you please. The money I'll
either give you cash each month or, should you prefer it, pay it into an
account. Oh, by the way, your Milton."

Panicked, I stumbled out of bed.

"I took the liberty," he smiled, "of placing it under lock and key
with the Blake. You know I have *The Marriage of Heaven and Hell*?
You'd like to see it, I suppose. Tonight, perhaps. A sharing of treasures.
I'll leave you the day to settle in."

He was gone and I was alone. Lying on the bed I noticed that the ceiling was conspicuously false. Made of scored pine and shaped into a mild funnel. Right in the center of it was a convex mirror about a foot wide. By the window were a desk and a chair, both mahogany, and a settee, faded and stained. I supposed it had originally been gray. Now it was a lot grayer. Bookcases. Polished wood. Reflecting glass.

I climbed into my clothes and found the bathroom. It was well provided and there was an opportunity for me to bathe if I chose to, but I didn't choose to. I made toast in the kitchen and some more coffee. On the table was a torn blue envelope with an American stamp. On it was written:

> The Archivist
> The Delaquay Society
> Beaumont Street
> Oxford
> England

I let myself out of the door and started walking the streets. The stones of Oxford may have been black but I would have been happy to number them as lovingly as Ruskin did those of Venice. Here was history, and no mistake. There was no escape from history, according to Grimshaw, but the Yorkshire moors tried their best sometimes. I didn't want to be on the edge of civilization, I wanted to be in the center of it.

I got round most of the colleges that day. Certainly by the end of the week I'd seen them all twice. In and out of chapels, peeping into halls and libraries. By the end of my first day I was pleasantly tired, and I was lying down on the gray sofa when Blanchard appeared again, through the door on the gallery.

"Settling in?" he shouted. "Be ready for dinner in an hour's time. Thought you should meet the librarian of the Isaac Lenau."

He disappeared back through his door. I thought I'd better go and take that bath after all.

When Blanchard next appeared with Donna beside him, I'd cleaned myself up and put on my one good suit. Just in time to be introduced. Grimshaw had been right to warn me. Women, I could see, might be a distraction.

It was a little restaurant just off the High. Though my French was good enough to understand the menu, I had no idea what anything might taste like. Agatha's cuisine could have remained happily untranslated as kitchen. I ordered the nearest thing I could see to steak and chips, then Blanchard took over. Wines were discussed and selected. As we raised our glasses, Blanchard toasted me.

"To young Tom, son of Tom, welcome to Oxford. This meal is courtesy of the Delaquay Society. Let us enjoy it."

Donna smiled at me. She was small, blond, blue-eyed, her hair brushed off her face. The dust of her face powder was set off dramatically by the mascara she had lavished on her eyelashes. Blanchard filled up my glass again. Nuits St.-Georges. Donna looked at me brightly.

"So you're coming to the Isaac Lenau?" she said.

"Yes. You're the librarian, Bill tells me."

"Assistant librarian, actually," she said, looking crossly at Blanchard. "The position of librarian in the Institute is a *very* prestigious one. After all, the Institute to all intents and purposes *is* a library."

Blanchard refilled her glass. "You will watch over him?" he said.

"I think Tom's quite capable of looking after himself. Aren't you, Tom?"

Blanchard filled my glass again. This was nice wine. The first I'd had, but the stuff struck me as very pleasant indeed. It gave me a warm thrumming sensation from my coccyx to my eyebrows. It had also begun to affect the muscles in my face, pressing my features inexorably toward a smile, which was directed consistently at Donna. She did not smile back, though, and it struck me as the evening deepened that she had a

secret grief, which I wished she would confide in me. My foot found
hers under the table. She looked at me without expression. Complicity.

Blanchard didn't exactly carry me home that night, but my arm was
round his neck and his arm was round my waist. My legs had started
moving independently, which struck me as wildly funny. I managed to
get right through "On Ilkley Moor baht 'at" twice—a bit of local color I
thought the cloisters might appreciate. After all, I'd been subjected to it
often enough to have it by heart and, technically speaking, I was American. Blanchard seemed relieved when he finally dropped me onto my
bed. He went out to make some coffee and I realized something about
Donna so profound that I knew I had to tell him, even though it might
be thought indiscreet. But by the time he'd come back, I'd passed out.

Sometime in the early hours of the morning, I woke to confusion,
headache, sharpening memories. Shame. Steamy shame. I had to apologize. Now. Quietly in the dark I made my way up the stairs to the gallery
and through the door. Moonlight from the large uncurtained windows
illuminated Blanchard's room. I made my way gently over to his bed.

It's odd, I suppose, but I'd always expected breasts to be more
sculptured and shaped than that, firmer, standing proud of the body.
More geometric almost. Donna's hair had fallen forward over her face. It
made her seem vulnerable. I almost reached out a hand to push it back
from her eyes.

I crept back out and down to my own bed. Blanchard should lock
that door really, I thought. I'd mention it. The next day, I'd have a word.

6

The Isaac Lenau Institute

We start out with a collector's mania to pursue these images. It is only toward the end that we come finally to understand: they have been pursuing us.
ISAAC LENAU, *Marginalia*, 377

"ISAAC LENAU WAS ONE OF THE GREAT MEN OF OUR TIME. HIS monument is here."

Dr. Lenski stopped and looked around the room. There were ten of us in there, on an odd assortment of folding chairs. The blind that hung over the window was broken.

"The Lenau Archive was saved from the Nazis by British generosity."

Again Lenski stopped and stared at us as though daring us to disagree.

"It is in some ways tragic that our Institute has always remained in temporary accommodation of one sort or another. Farringdon. Ealing. And now here. But at least we have kept the library together."

Lenski banged his hand down on the lectern as though he had won a point in a public debate and could now expect some applause. He was small and fat. His gray hair was cropped like a Roman emperor's. His three-piece suit, a brown tweed he may have thought was in the style of a country gentleman, was old and too tight for him. I found my eyes returning to the buttons of his waistcoat, as he gesticulated furiously with his hands. I had the odd fancy that if all the buttons were to fly off he would deflate suddenly like a ruptured balloon or a torn dirigible.

"The library is Lenau's work. The Archive is the library. His notes were written inside the books, around the margins, across the title pages and endpapers. Even between the lines. So his work, you see, was inseparable from the library, *is* the library. We're now reasonably confident that all his commentary has been separately printed in the Journals of the Lenau Archive—but, you see, its very separation from the texts by which it was nourished somehow weakens it. It is my personal opinion that Lenau himself would probably not have allowed the separation. But, alas! he is not here to tell us."

Lenski paused here and turned to the window. He marched over to it, picked up the pole at its side, and stabbed the broken blind with some vehemence. This made it drop down a little further, and even more lopsidedly than before. He slammed the pole back against the wall in disgust and returned to the lectern. He tried to smile but his mouth merely twitched, as though afflicted with a rictus.

"Temporary accommodation, as I said. For twenty years we've been shifted from one set of lodgings to another. We are, grateful, of course. Don't misunderstand me.

"You must spend your first week here attending all the lectures— one each day—and studying the library, its manner of classification, the tree-file index. This is not like any other library. The foundation of Lenau's work was tracing the lineage of images, backward and forward in time, across cultures.

"You might, for example, look up madness and find yourself surprised to be directed to a small book on mimicry by a Swiss theologian and Lenau's commentary inside it. The card-insert would then inform you that Lenau himself was incarcerated in an asylum at the time he was writing in the book. He was himself insane, at that point. That was the official description and he never disputed it. He came back, he said, chastened by the perceptions of the damned. He needed to make that journey to understand how often the gestures and iconography of the mad was mimicry: the mimicking of their tormentors in an attempt to speak their language and thus gain release from their persecution. The lineaments of primitive terror can be traced through history. History, according to Lenau, consists of the traces in the sand we have left in our struggle to overcome or at least mitigate that terror. The terror returns always in new forms. New forms and old. Maenads. Storm troopers. Lenau's suicide, remember, was his response to the latest form it was taking there and then out on the streets. . . .

"The card-insert will also direct you to *King Lear,* to Edgar's beggar and the contemporary exorcisms Shakespeare alluded to in that play. It will point you simultaneously to Bedlam and the spectacle it afforded an Elizabethan audience on their leisure days; and to Hamlet and his protest at having his stops known, his mystery plucked out. Then it will send you to the illustrated books and Lenau's annotations on them. To Medusa's face in Perseus's shield, the annihilating image tempered to an icon. Exorcised, as it were, in metals or in oils. To the Bacchae who tore Pentheus apart, even though he had dressed as one of them, put on their uniform. He attempted the disguise of their normality, but it didn't save him.

"I will read you finally, if you will permit me, Lenau's gloss on his copy of Baudelaire:

"What is the age dressed in? The modern age enters the stage clothed in the rags of the chiffonnier. He is dressed up in the patched cloth of previous ages. A motley of allusion. Tradition's ruins. This actor has in consequence the simultaneous appearance of being everyone and no one. He is left to glean the detritus of his own progress."

Lenski stopped and stared at the ten of us for a moment.

"Ladies and gentlemen," he said, "welcome once more to the Isaac Lenau Institute. We'll probably make more rapid progress if you kindly leave your preconceptions at the door."

At lunch the conversation was subdued. It was difficult for any of us to say much about Lenski's talk because I don't think any of us understood it. You could see the doubts already beginning in some faces as they asked themselves what they had let themselves in for. Things did not improve after lunch.

We were led to the lecture room, which was as ramshackle and nondescript as the reception hall had been. After a few minutes a tall woman entered, draped from her neck to her feet in black with a shawl about her shoulders. She was thin, consumptively thin and white. Her hair was dark and fell down free below her shoulders. No comb had interfered with it for some time.

"Rachel Fein," the woman sitting next to me whispered. "Won't use soap, won't eat meat."

"I am Dr. Fein," she had begun, looking at us all bleakly. "I will explain to you something about images in your work here. How you are to use them, how not."

Her English, though proper, was that of someone who spoke other languages more naturally.

"First a warning about photographs. We are only interested in photography here insofar as it aids the *artistic* evidence. We do not imagine that if we had a photograph of Picasso's weeping woman, for example, we would therefore have a truer picture of her than the painter's canvas. We would be inclined to say the opposite. Similarly with these pictures."

She lifted up a large board which had on it pairs of images, photographs matched with reproductions of paintings. A little thud in my heart registered that one of them was Turner's painting of Bolton Abbey. The painting was famous enough but I hadn't expected it to come back and meet me so soon.

"Look at these Turners, for example. There is one here of Pembroke Castle and one of . . ." She bent down to read the note, and I blurted out "Bolton Abbey."

She looked at me with interest. "You are right," she said. "Good. Look at the paintings carefully and then the photographs. In the camera's account of the same terrain there are differences. Turner has shifted the water and hills to obtain his particular effects. This he did all the time. In 1804 the Oxford Almanac refused to take his picture of Balliol, pointing out that the sun appeared to be shining from the northeast. But we are not a school of historical topography, we are an art institute. We have no particular interest in the eye of the camera, which is monocular, Cyclopean, mechanical. If we start with a specific topographic deposition in the Turners, three lenses have rearranged it: binocular vision and the imagination. If you wish to use the word 'distortion' here, remember that you have then ventured into the psychology of art. What is being distorted and toward what does the distortion aspire? To the ideal? Away from it? Are we sure we know what the ideal is? If Raphael should see no creases in the flesh of a female model, and Rembrandt should see nothing but creases, who then distorts?

"It will be necessary for you to examine your vocabulary closely. Avoid if possible the use of words like 'influence.' A moment's consideration will usually establish that the word prevents thought on the very subject it was meant to address. Let me give you a little example from an area that Lenau himself addressed and constantly reverted to.

"What is the relation of the Quattrocento to antiquity? Was it shaped by it? Hindered by it? Provoked by it? Did it merely appropriate it and, if so, then what was it before it did the appropriating? Did a Gothic dragon swallow classical antiquity and find the Renaissance in its womb? You might quickly come to the conclusion that you can't answer these questions but at least you won't throw words like 'influence' around.

"You might think instead, as Lenau often did, of a fundamental intellectual asymmetry at the heart of the Judaeo-Christian tradition. This God, as Pascal reminded us, is antipathetic to the gods of the philosophers. Such asymmetry finds its way into the iconographic tradition but yearns, as all imbalance however dynamic does, for rest and composure. The symmetry of the classical with its counterbalanced deities inevitably attracts it. Then soon enough the turbulence of the Baroque wishes to escape the symmetry. The angels try to flap their plaster wings and fly."

I was taking notes when Dr. Fein started talking but soon stopped. I had no way of following the connections she was making. Nothing at Southwell had prepared me for this. She didn't appear to use any notes herself. She kept a large illustrated book open in front of her on the desk. Sometimes she would stop and turn the pages. When a particular image caught her, then she was off again, talking at speed from a script that seemed already written. Her long, thin fingers clawed the air for emphasis.

The woman beside me was cross. "Did you understand that? I couldn't follow a single word of what she was blathering on about. I think my father might have been right about this place, after all."

She wouldn't be long here, I suspected. The mysteriousness that intrigued me obviously repelled her. I made for the library.

They had kept the only three large rooms in the building for this. It was impressive and its system of classification, as we had been warned, seemed entirely baffling. On one shelf the labels read "Wings—primitive—classical—medieval—Renaissance—Enlightenment—modern." On another: "Chrysalis—consumption for resurrection in early mythology."

Donna was sitting writing card-indexes at a table by the window. I walked slowly toward her and leaned my head down until she had seen me. A smile.

"Tom. Finding your way around?"

"Yes," I whispered. "I've been lectured to by Dr. Lenski and Dr. Fein."

"And lived to tell the tale."

"I'm trying to work out what I should be reading. No one's mentioned that."

"No, they wouldn't," she said, her smile disappearing. "There's only one problem with this place—nobody runs it. Oh, various eminences *administer* it, but no one actually runs it. Come here."

She took me by the hand and led me to a shelf entitled simply "Memory." She took down a battered volume and handed it to me.

"Read that," she said, "it'll get you started."

I looked at the book in my hands and opened it at the title page:

The Sustaining Wound
A Meditation on Memory
by
Giles Astley
1907

I closed it and looked at Donna, who was running her fingers along the spines of the books on the shelf.

"I'm sorry about last night," I whispered. "I think I might have had a bit too much to—"

She looked around the library quickly then leaned over without a word and kissed me. On the lips.

Back at the flat, I opened Astley's book and started reading:

It was with the genius of a poet that John Keats opened The Fall of Hyperion *at the shrine of Mnemosyne. This goddess, mother of all nine muses, is simultaneously giving and unforgiving. Keats calls her "The pale omega of a withered race"—a line both instinct with beauty and preternaturally apt, for memory consists of the characters incised inside us. The alphabet of recollection is cut through trauma—the trauma of pleasure as well as pain.*

Any experience which is too large to simply pass through the portals of the waking mind inflicts a wound. This wound is runic; the inscriptional store which is the sum total of all such wounds is what we call memory. The written form is memory discarnate from its original victim: a memory from which the recorder has vanished. What sustains here are not the participants of recollection, but the deposit left us later. In this sense of course memory is history and history may be deemed to include pre-history, if those

*scratchings and scrapings over stones on bleak moorsides might
be regarded as a proto-alphabet, the first ill-fashioned letters of a
child's script. . . .*

My head came up off the page and was confronted with the Cow
and Calf rocks at Ilkley. They were less than half a mile from Southwell
and I used to go there often. "Those stones have power," Grimshaw
used to say, but he didn't have to tell me that. In the quarry at dawn or
dusk there'd be rabbits, pigeons, a kestrel. The top of the valley here
rubbed shoulders with the clouds: it was as high as the weather. A natural place for worship. They lit fires there. At dawn they must have seen
what I saw: after a night of rain a powder blue sky over the reds, browns,
and greens of the moor. And, always, the gray of the rock. (Only its skin
was gray. After a rockfall you'd see the rich dark yellow of the grit with
feldspar and quartz scattered through it. Why did I ever say Yorkshire
was in black and white? And yet it was too, if memory's archive's to be
believed.)

They had scratched and chiseled at the stone in the most exposed
places. Right on the edges where the wind could slap you sideways to
your death. Cups and rings, the antiquarians had called them. No one
knew why or what for. Some grew so exasperated by the unreadiness of
these markings to yield meaning, they blamed the weather. A freak signature of gales and rain.

I put my fingers in the grooves and traced the shapes as though they
were Braille chipped into Mosaic tablets. At the swastika stone, which I
trekked to once a week, I traced the interlocking patterns round and
round again. This swastika was not the geometric hard-angled one of the
Nazis—the lines were rounded, almost organic, as though it represented
some primitive four-legged form of life ready to run back into the cave
of the past. Or an early essay at the starfish, wheeling through salty
murk. And the Cow Stone looking down on it was, from the southeast
anyway, a sphinx. They had crouched on the sphinx's shoulders carving

those messages we couldn't understand. On the scarp side of the valley a glacier had cut. Where the moorland met the sky.

Fingers on my neck. Blanchard. He came around in front of me grinning. He was drinking whiskey. He held out the glass toward me.

"Like one?"

I shook my head. He leaned over the book.

"Ah yes, Astley. Memories as wounds. A work passed over in silence these days, except for the strange creatures at the Lenau. Get anything?"

"Yes," I said, then I stopped. Without knowing why I suddenly went on, "I've not told the truth about my mother."

Blanchard's grin grew wider then exploded in a laugh.

"We none of us do, dear boy, believe me."

I hadn't told the truth about her, though. Not even to myself. Beneath the skin of the rock, it was all a different color.

7

Wittgenstein's Disciple

*The most beautiful philosophic statement ever made has never
cost the earth a single tree. It was the silence of Saint Thomas
Aquinas after he had put his words away and stared into the light
that surrounded him.*
ALFRED DELAQUAY, *Diaries*

I SUPPOSE I FELL FOR BILL AS SOON AS I SAW HIM ON THAT STATION
platform, so happy in the rain. He always had this smile on his face as
though he had just discovered the meaning of life and found it was, if
not a joke exactly, certainly less serious than everyone had been led to
believe previously. I started to compare myself with Bill but that didn't
work. To begin with I was five or six inches shorter and skinny to the
point of shame, where he had the build of a natural athlete. And his chin
was dark from shaving, where I didn't need to shave at all. Once a week
I'd scrape the steel over my face but only as a gesture to my own man-
hood. There was no real need.

I stood naked in front of the bathroom mirror and pondered. The
problem seemed, on the surface anyway, irresolvable. No amount of natural development or athletic training would bridge the gap between us.
But when we went out together and he put his arm around my shoulder,
I felt he'd made me his equal. I suppose, to be fair to myself, my
upbringing had been a little strange—Grimshaw including me in the
frenzy of his own obsessions. Agatha would watch me all the time but
when we occasionally made physical contact it was like colliding with a

tool bag, canvas-cold and iron-jointed. She wore her Emily Dickinson hairdo like a reproach to the gossiping world outside.

That Saturday evening Bill came whistling down the steps and said we should buy some fish and chips, then go for a drink in Jericho.

"You haven't eaten?"

"No," I said.

"Good. Don't waste too much time in the kitchen. Wittgenstein lived on sandwiches from Woolworth's for years. Didn't mind what he ate as long as it didn't stop him working and was exactly the same each time. Differences between meals distracted him."

The blankness of my face snagged him.

"Wittgenstein? Ludwig Wittgenstein? Not one of Grimshaw's specialties, I suppose. Too busy talking about Thomas Aquinas. I'll fill you in as we go."

We bought fish and chips and ate them out of damp, hot newspapers with the vinegar slowly soaking through.

"The thing is," Bill started, still juggling a hot chip in his mouth, "I'd studied philosophy, but I'd never studied with a philosopher. Oh, I grant you, one professor had written three books on ethics and epistemology and another had written the definitive study of the utilitarian mind, but they weren't . . . somehow . . . philosophers. They just philosophized. Actually, there's something inherently disgusting about being a don who philosophizes, but let that pass for the moment.

"Wittgenstein at Cambridge was the real thing. He had already created one philosophic method with the *Tractatus*. Put Russell out of business with that—well, logically anyway. Then he cleared off out of academia altogether, exactly at the point where any of my professors would have cashed in. A gardener in a monastery. A primary-school teacher half a mile from nowhere. I admired that, you see. When he started teaching again at Cambridge, and word was out that he was up to something new, I went there. Asked if I could sit in on his tutorials. Yes, he said. Well, he didn't say no.

"Nothing like them. Nothing like them before or since. This wasn't the port-brained enigma of the high table. This wasn't thesis-grooming. Here was real thought at the cutting edge. Sharp as a razor. Occam's. What does this *mean*? Taught me to understand that philosophy is no more than one expression of a system of life, an organization of beings, a mode of existence. Not even a particularly important one, in Wittgenstein's view, though he agonized over getting it right and was always on the point of giving it up."

Bill took the last chip and dipped it in the little pool of vinegar in the paper and then, as though it were an animal he'd caught after a ceremonial hunt, he raised it in the air and dropped it tail-first into his upturned mouth. He rolled the newspaper into a ball and threw it hard into the forecourt of the University Press building we were walking past.

"Wouldn't publish my book." He grinned. "Or Grimshaw's."

In the pub I bought the pints. Bill had found a table and was sitting there with his index finger pushed hard up his left nostril. When he took it down there was a black ball on the end of it that he carefully flicked at the ceiling. He saw me looking at him with disbelief and smiled:

> *"The angelical doctor Aquinas*
> *Traced an itch heading north up his sinus*
> *So he didn't malinger*
> *He inserted a finger*
> *It's intentional acts that define us.*

"It's my ambition," he went on, "to write the history of western philosophy in limerick form. It would constitute a kind of mnemonic. Consult your Astley."

I took my packet of Craven "A" from my pocket and offered him one. We lit up. I had taken Bill's advice and decided to have a positive attitude to these things. I still felt a little sick toward the bottom end of each cigarette, but I was studying Bill's gestures with them, how he waved one in the air to clinch a point, or sometimes bent his head down into the smoke as though disappearing for a moment to consider things. There was an intellectual theatricality about his smoking that I was attempting to imitate.

"The problem you're going to have to face before too long about your Grimshaw inheritance is this. The old man's right that the English Reformation was an act of state, that the dissolution was theft, that saintly men and women died in protest against it. But he forgets the other side. Does he think Jesus built the Catholic Church on the evening of the Last Supper? Does he think the good Lord himself dropped down and started up half the superstitious twaddle that's traveled in the name of that religion all these centuries? He never thinks hard enough about the sincerity of the reformers themselves—their detestation of the gimcrack rituals so often peddled in the streets and chapels in the name of the religion of Rome.

"All religions are corrupt, corrupted by greed for certainty and fear of the unknown."

"And the wish to find protection," I said.

"You mean the Nazi business? Yes, he has no illusions there, that's for sure. Grimshaw's not an easy man to summarize."

The next morning I went to mass at Blackfriars. It was simple and white inside and the Dominicans sang the plainchant well. And when I went up to take the wafer in my mouth I felt, as I always did, momentarily voided and renewed, but I sensed that all I believed would be assailed in this place I had come to.

When I arrived back, Bill was sitting at the table with books before him.

"I've been looking through the Milton. And look, Tom, here's my Blake. *The Marriage of Heaven and Hell.* You've not seen it yet, with all the excitement. Come and find out a little about contrariness."

I sat down on the other chair. Bill turned the pages. He started to read aloud:

"As I was walking among the fires of hell, delighted with the enjoyments of Genius, which to Angels look like torment and insanity, I collected some of their Proverbs; thinking that as the sayings used in a nation mark its character, so the Proverbs of Hell shew the nature of Infernal wisdom better than any description of buildings or garments.

"When I came home: on the abyss of the five senses, where a flat-sided steep frowns over the present world, I saw a mighty Devil folded in black clouds, hovering on the sides of the rock, with corroding fires he wrote the following sentence now perceived by the minds of men, & read by them on earth:

"'How do you know but ev'ry Bird that cuts the airy way,
Is an immense world of delight, clos'd by your senses five?'"

I recognized the face of the devil Delaquay had drawn. It had the same tortured features as the one of Satan I had spent so much time drawing. I pointed to it.

"Satan," I said.

Bill started laughing.

"No, no, no," he said. "That's one of the angels tormented by the works of genius. Here's the devil, over here."

On the other side was a luminous figure, shining with divine intelligence.

"But he doesn't look damned," I said.

"Maybe he isn't," Bill said. "For Blake the contraries are inseparable. The prolific and the devourer. The building of the imagination collapsing into the ruins of law." He lit a cigarette then handed it to me to smoke while he lit another.

"You'll have to forget what you think you know of the law to read Blake. How much do you know about Delaquay?"

"Not much. Grimshaw said he met him. Is that true?"

"Right at the end, yes. But by then . . . Well, come up here and look at some things."

I followed him up the steps and through into his rooms. Over in the far corner beyond the bed, which was still unmade, there was a glass-fronted bookcase. Bill took the key out of his pocket and opened it. On the top shelf was a row of leather-bound books, thick and bulky like law manuals. Each had the initials D.P. embossed in gold on the spine and underneath them the year, 1895, say, or 1914.

"These contain all that's ever been written about Delaquay," he said. "All that's of any worth anyhow. Every paper of the Society, you understand. There are others from outside who write sometimes, having been shown things they should probably never have seen. But here's all you'll find of any value.

"There are different interpretations, you see. Maybe there are even different Delaquays, who knows? But you should at least know of the Dark Theory. Otherwise there'll be no point you even looking at his Baudelaire."

Bill took out the volume marked D.P. 1919 and gave it to me.

"Don't take it out of the building," he said. "There are people who'd like to get their hands on these things. There is a . . . well, never mind—you have enough to be thinking about as it is."

I carried the book back down to my own rooms. So on my desk now I had Delaquay's Milton and his Blake and the writings of the Dark Theorists.

That evening Bill came and sat on the bed smoking.

"I'm going away for a few weeks," he said. "I'm committed to a number of things. I'll leave you the key to the Delaquay bookcase. Here. Keep things locked up. Donna may come and go. She has her own key to the place."

I looked at him in silence.

"They're not all like your mother," he said, "whatever she was like. Stop worrying about it. It's certainly no harder than learning to smoke."

∎

Bill had gone by the time I left for the Lenau on Monday. The lecture that day was by Rachel Fein: "Pathos and Sympathy: How the gods move." She was wrapped in her mummy cloths as usual, with the black shawl which slipped from her shoulders as she spoke. She seemed even thinner and whiter than usual, a ghost with articulate fingers.

"What we find on the walls which the Egyptians carved and painted is not stylistic primitivism, but a priority of information over what we call realism. The legs sideways, the torso turned toward us, the face in profile, the feet portrayed from the insole whether left or right. This allows for a maximum of information to be conveyed. If we choose to portray what the eye can see at any one time, foreshortening feet and arms in the process, that is not a superior style, merely one with an exaggerated fidelity to the moment of perception. Socrates spoke of showing how the feelings affect the body in movement and so reveal the soul. One must wish, of course, to have the soul revealed. Not all cultures do. Some would regard it as an obscenity.

"Pathos is movement. It is passion shaken free out of stasis. It must either portray a departure from harmonic symmetry or convey a possible return to it. Otherwise the movement itself is unintelligible. That which is portrayed or presented is, of course, remade, it is re-presented. This is the impulse behind the anti-iconic commandments of the Jews. For them the sacred was for the tongue and the ear, not the eye.

"Unlike the classical Greeks and Romans, for the Jews God speaks through the human body, the human face, the human voice—hence the prophets. He speaks as the living God, not through copies of the living God. There is a great prohibition on the making or copying of images of divinity. What God has once made, only profane men seek to remake. What can be uttered over and over—and indeed must be—is the word of God. Experience cannot be recapitulated, only enacted. To recapitulate suggests a cyclic view of history appropriate to paganism and idolatry. God's relation to his people here is dynamic, ongoing. It is not history which must return upon itself but the people who must return to God. Yet what they must return to cannot even be uttered. The sacred name cannot be spoken. *Hashem,* we say, the name.

"Here, you see, a visual depiction of the sacred is not merely theft but blasphemy, sacrilege. We can see a parallel perhaps with the so-called primitive fear of images. Draw a man's sheep and you have taken ownership of them. Draw his wife and you have committed fornication. Make an image of him and burn it, you have invoked his death. Think carefully, all of you, about these maneuvers of the mind, for they are none of them irrelevant to what we have come to study.

"Now look at these pictures."

She held up one of her boards, on which were taped a picture of a cross and a picture of a swastika.

"What are they?" she said.

A voice from the front said, "A cross and a swastika."

"But what *are* they? What do they have in common?"

I lifted my hand up gently. She nodded at me and that torrent of hair started again down her face.

"Symbols," I said.

"Good. They are signs. They are symbols. What is the basic definition of a symbol?"

Again there was a silence and again my hand moved up, as all of Grimshaw's sessions on the sacraments came back to me.

"One thing which is made to stand for another. Something which stands for a meaning which is not inherent in it."

Rachel Fein's look was as sharp as her fingernails.

"Good," she said. "So here now. Look. Two pieces of wood nailed together. It could be a strengthener for the gable end of a building. It could be a post to hang dead foxes on. But a man was put on one of these, as part of the routine torture of the Roman empire two thousand years ago, and now it means . . . redemption, salvation. Well, for some, anyway.

"And this," she said, pointing to the swastika, "does anyone know what this originally meant?"

It seemed to be my day for answers, so I started again.

"Well-being and good fortune. It was the sign of the worshipers of light."

She looked at me again with her finger flat against her lips. "Yes, but no one needs asking what it means now. This symbol was taken over and remade. It represents the opposite of what the other one means. Damnation, destruction. Well, for some, anyway.

"See how you must put the visual into question. When we talk of provenance here we are not interested in who owned the picture. We are referring to its intellectual provenance. We want to know the economy of belief and instruction out of which it arose. Now look here."

She lifted up another of her boards. There were three pictures on it. She pointed to the first. It was one of those seventeenth-century paintings of a man surrounded by his paintings, row upon row of them hanging on his walls.

"In one word," she said, "what are we instructed to look at?"

"Collector," I said, growing overconfident.

"Not quite," she said. "Possession."

"Now this," she said, pointing to a photograph of sacred pictures on the walls of what looked like a monastery.

"I'll help you a little. These are the paintings of Fra Angelico in the monastery of San Marco in Firenze. One word."

"Religion," said a voice from behind me.

"Let's say devotion," she said.

"Now this." She pointed to the third illustration. It was a silk scroll of a mountain. Chinese. With characters brushed eloquently down the side.

"Let me help you a little. It was kept scrolled away and only taken out to be looked at. The ideograms are a poem and they describe the interaction of moonlight and the mountain."

"Meditation," I said, confident again.

"Meditation, yes. So there we are, then. Three types of art with three different intentions. All of them may have started out from what we call the sacred, but see what different uses they employ, what different responses they demand. Should we be moved, then? To be moved is to respond to the absence of stillness. To be moved is to undergo passion. In the Christian tradition the ultimate passion is the passion of Christ, before which our sympathy—our joint suffering—must lead on to devotion. For the Chinese artist who made this silk, we should empty ourselves of passion, forget the false gods of movement. And for the figure in this other picture the gold in our purse corresponds to the truth in our hearts. What we see in pictures will depend on what we remember and what we remember will depend on who we are."

She put her boards together and walked to the door. On the way out I thought she smiled at me.

I spent much of the week pursuing those three different elements she'd spoken about. I found a little book on San Marco and studied it: a house of belief whose walls were filled with images. It made me think of Grimshaw's house in Ilkley.

8

The Dark Theory

"I have cultivated my hysteria with ecstasy and terror."
CHARLES BAUDELAIRE, *Journaux Intimes*

THAT FRIDAY NIGHT I FINALLY SAT DOWN WITH THE DELAQUAY
Proceedings. I went up into Bill's apartment and poured myself a glass
of his whiskey. As payment, I made his bed.

It was a beautiful book. I suppose nothing connected with this particular obsession was going to be less than beautiful. I flipped through
some of the bibliographies and minutes of meetings until I came to the
essay entitled "A Dark Proposal: Delaquay's Paris Years." I lit a cigarette, took a sip of the whiskey, and started to read.

The Paris of the Third Republic which Delaquay inhabited was a
place of ultimate contradictions. The extreme skeptical rationalism
inaugurated by the Revolution was counterpointed by a supernat-
uralism of demonic intent. We know sufficient of the goings-on
involving such names as Huysmans, Rémy de Gourmont, and
Eliphas Lévi to have no doubt that diabolism and Satanism were
certainly current at the time. Some have had difficulties taking
such material seriously. What can no longer be in doubt after the
recent discovery of Delaquay's diaries from the 1890s is how seri-
ously he himself took them.

The demonic and the damned appear throughout Delaquay's
work. The School of Contrariety holds that he was engaging
here in a type of dialectical thought, not unlike the Blake of

The Marriage of Heaven and Hell. *This, we must now acknowl-edge, is too glib a position. The tortured quality of the illustra-tions matches the tortured quality of Delaquay's own life and mind. We have this now on his own authority. In his own words, he scoured the depths, and the depths infected him.*

As a result of his inheritance, Delaquay was, of course, of independent means. He had no need to do anything he did not choose to do. And he had lost his faith. He did not, however, believe in the scientific materialism of his day, nor did he care for naturalism in the arts. In some ways he has much in common with Baudelaire, though it was perhaps his friendship with Huys-mans which was more influential in prompting him to take what he later called "the dark road."

There is no question that he attended at least one black mass, probably in the same chapel in the rue de Sèvres which Huysmans himself frequented. There can be little question either, given the iconography so prevalent throughout both his edition of Les Fleurs du mal *and his* Là Bas, *that he witnessed the desecration of the host. The chasuble portraying a black goat and the naked celebrant inside it could have been inventions but they have about them an uncanny conviction which makes one wonder whether they were based on observation. If so, then we are in the same world as that portrayed in an article in* Le Matin *in May 1899, where a black mass was reported in all its squalid detail. This was reported to have taken place in the Quartier Saint-Sulpice. In that report there was also an account of an aged cele-brant, a disgraced priest of some notoriety, naked inside his chasuble. A litany of obscenity and curses proceeded from the cel-ebrant's mouth. Desecrated hosts bearing the sigils of demons were fed to white rats. At the end of the ceremony, when the orgy was beginning, the reporter fled—in some terror according to his own accounts.*

There are many summaries of the extent of these activities.
Arthur Edward Waite's Devil Worship in France, *London 1896,*
is one of the more reliable. A little livelier, though less scholarly,
is Le Satanisme et la magie *by Jules Bois. What we are pointing*
out here is that Delaquay moved in a society where such encoun-
ters were not necessarily unusual. In a strange and unexpected
extension of the spirit of 1789, evocation had become democ-
ratized.

When Baudelaire says, "J'ai cultivé mon hysterie avec jouis-
sance et terreur," we should attend to what he says. An ecstatic,
indulgent delight and the terror that attended upon it were what
the participants of these activities let themselves in for. But what
of the hysteria? Charcot's practice in Paris had thrown up the pos-
sibility that all such visions, that all apparent encounters with the
demonic, were no more than hallucinations. And if they were
hallucinations then they were prompted by repressed desire. If
this were the case, then intellectual bravery demanded that one
explore such experiences for oneself. Delaquay took that position,
or at least convinced himself that he had for a while.

The fear and menace of his work during this period certainly
do not show much evidence of delight. He moved on from
hashish to morphine, which he injected three times a day. If his
vision became delirious, it was delirious with exactitude, and this
was an infernal precision. If what he saw was not real in any
objective sense, then his imagination made it so. It became a part
of Delaquay's belief that heaven and hell co-existed in the same
room and he quoted the rabbinic commentary Yalkut Koheleth
to the effect that the two realms of heaven and hell are only a
hand-breadth apart.

His final denunciation of the Satanists, after his own terrible
breakdown, led to the psychic assaults upon him which he
believed they orchestrated and which, he maintained until the

end of his days, had threatened his life. The figure of the succubus, which appears at this point, recurs throughout his work in a number of ambiguous contexts. This attacking but seductive female figure became a kind of inverted icon in the margins of his work.

One result of this part of his life which has not previously been remarked upon is his fascination with the strange claims of Diana Vaughan. Though it was announced in the June 1895 issue of Revue Mensuelle *that this lady had been received into the Catholic Church, she had previously made the remarkable claim that Henry Vaughan, the seventeenth-century mystic and poet, had consummated a mystical marriage with Venus-Astarte and had practiced black magic.*

This claim, regarded as dubious in the extreme even at the time, appears to have inspired some of the illustrations in Delaquay's edition of Vaughan's 1650 book, Silex Scintillans. *The following lines about Isaac are particularly relevant:*

> *But thou a chosen sacrifice wert given*
> *And offered up so early unto heaven*
> *Thy flames could not be out; Religion was*
> *Rayed into thee, like beams into a glass,*
> *Where, as thou grewst, it multiplied and shined,*
> *The sacred constellation of thy mind.*

The rubric alters with the phrase "Thy flames could not be out," and Delaquay was driven to a curious visual extremity in his illustration. In the Zohar *it is written in regard to Abraham and Isaac and the sacrifice: "The Deviser of Evil always appears behind things and words; he comes to challenge." In cabbalistic teaching Isaac represents judgment. He brings rigor to Abraham, who had previously lacked it. The demonic forces are always threatening. Evil can never be escaped, it must always be encountered.*

Delaquay has shown this very possibility of evil shining through Isaac's head, shining through that sacred constellation of his mind. According to the cabbala, Isaac was not a boy when he was taken to the mountain. He was thirty-seven. Delaquay published his edition of Vaughan in 1899, when he himself was thirty-seven. The colophon of that book enclosed two sigils, one ∿ denoting Amenadiel, who announces secrets to the west and has three hundred servants; the other ⌇ Demoriel, who announces secrets to the north and has four hundred servants. The sigils thus spell out the initials of the name Alfred Delaquay. In the preface which Delaquay wrote (uniquely) for this book he said: "Northwest of here in England lived a poet once, whose spiritual insight has not been surpassed in the seven hundred years since Dante."

There is a point when apparently fortuitous detail accrues into a pattern which can no longer be ignored. Part of the problem in our opinion has been that by viewing Delaquay's work backward from the achieved serenity of his Tempest *and* Gospel of John, *we minimize the reality of the dark years and his own complete involvement in the themes of darkness. In the diaries we have been making use of here there is a statement from 1899 which should give us all pause: "Satanism is an affirmation of the divine order."*

Then I read the Delaquay edition of *The Marriage of Heaven and Hell.* By the time I had finished it I had lost my faith. Let me perhaps put that another way. By the time I had finished it I had removed the circumference of law from my faith. I had ceased in my devotion to constraint. I was utterly convinced of the rightness of what Blake was saying. Never has any piece of writing so entirely convinced me of its truth. And its truth received further illumination from those astonishing images from Delaquay. There were two in particular to which I kept turning back. One illustrated the line "He whose face gives no Light, shall never become a star" and the image of darkness and cancellation which Delaquay had conjured from that seemed to me a true image of damnation. The other was against this passage:

> *By degrees we beheld the infinite Abyss, fiery as the smoke of a burning city; beneath us, at an immense distance, was the sun, black but shining; round it were fiery tracks on which revolv'd vast spiders, crawling after their prey, which flew, or rather swam, in the infinite deep, in the most terrific shapes of animals sprung from corruption; & the air was full of them, seem'd composed of them: they are Devils, and are called Powers of the air. I now asked my companion which was my eternal lot? He said: "Between the black and white spiders."*

Opposite this was an engraving far more complex than any I had seen previously by Delaquay. It reminded me if anything of Bosch and of the weird hybrids that tortured each other in hell or tormented the desert penances of Saint Anthony. But there was a face I recognized in the midst of the swarm of black and white spiders. Thin, pale, bearded and with wide, haunted eyes. I opened up the Delaquay Proceedings again and there it was—the photograph of Delaquay taken in 1900. This was his self-portrait. A self-portrait in hell. But if this was Blake's hell, and I understood Blake aright, it was in truth heaven. Why then was the expression on his face so tormented?

I had brought my drawing materials with me from Ilkley and I started to draw what Delaquay had drawn before me. I was driven with a frenzy I'd not known before. In the years since Grimshaw had first put that devil face before me and challenged me to capture it, I had drawn Delaquay over and over. Not copied him, that would be the wrong word for, stung by Grimshaw's criticisms of my first attempts, I had tried to find something of my own in this activity. In the process I had learned much of Delaquay's own technique, his way with a line, the curious drama of his cross-hatching, the scurry of black with which he shaded. Sometimes I would try subjects of my own, but they always seemed lifeless, as though only with the Delaquays before me did my hand touch fire.

I drew through the whole of that Saturday. Sometimes I stopped and read the text again from beginning to end. Sometimes I poured myself more of Bill's whiskey (I noticed how low the bottle was getting) but always back to this task. Who was I trying to find? Blake? Delaquay? Myself?

I was bent over the table scratching with one of Grimshaw's old pens when her fingers traced a line along the back of my neck. She leaned over and her cheek touched my ear. Donna.

"That is good. That is very good indeed. I wouldn't have known. Does anyone know you can do that?"

Her perfume, some moorland heathery scent. The stiffness of her dress where it covered her breasts.

"How did you ever learn to do that?"

"Years of looking at them," I said. "They were my holy pictures. Or maybe my unholy ones. At my bedside."

She had come through silently from Bill's rooms. She already had a whiskey in her hand. The bottle would be lower still.

"Don't stop," she said. "I'll be up there when you finish. Did you make Bill's bed?"

I nodded.

"I thought so. The first time I've ever known it."

I carried on but my concentration was gone. I laid them down on the table side by side and looked at them. She was right. They were good. Better than anything I'd ever done. None of them were quite the same as the images they had started out from, that was the point. They hadn't copied anything except the style. And the passion. They were as good as his.

I carried them up through the gallery. She was sitting curled up on the bed with one of the D.P. volumes open on the pillow. Black stockings.

Bare white arms. The whiskey bottle was empty. She must have had another. Yellow hair. A lioness at her siesta. Her nails were long and painted red. I handed the drawings to her.

"You are clever," she said, and hummed a little. "So very clever. Someone so clever can take me to dinner. On your vast allowance from the Delaquay Society."

I'd not thought much about money, but she assured me I had enough that I needn't worry. She also told me to bring the checkbook that Bill had given me. We would go to the same restaurant where we had been before, she said. They were always happy to receive a D.S. check there.

On the way she slipped her arm through mine. Should I think about Bill? He wasn't the law, and even if he was I had just learned from Blake that the law was the line that reason drew around energy. When we arrived I smoked ostentatiously until the first course arrived. I ordered the usual wine. Perhaps I had been right the first time we had sat at different sides of this table. Complicity. How old was she? No way of knowing. It didn't matter.

"You'll be in great demand at the Lenau if word of your talent gets about."

"Will I?" I said, angling my cigarette down from my fingers thoughtfully. "It's no good them asking me to do Rembrandt or Ingres. I can only do Delaquay. Can't even draw a convincing cabbage otherwise."

"How intriguing," she said. The strange thing was, I think she meant it. She seemed so much less distracted without Bill around.

"It was Grimshaw—my headmaster, well, I suppose my guardian really. It was his obsession. One of them. I picked it up from him. Now it's become a part of my mind."

"You sound as though you regret it," she said. "You shouldn't. It's a rare gift. Some would envy you."

"Do you?"

"I envy you a lot more than you could imagine. A lot more."

The soups came. Then the steaks. We finished the wine. We had a coffee and a brandy. It was only nine o'clock.

"You could take me for a nightcap in the Lamb and Flag," she said brightly.

One of the nicest things about Donna was her height—I towered over her. This time I put my arm around her shoulder, as Bill would often lay his arm across mine. What was it stiffened her hair like that, made it like feathery corn or some exotic plumage? Her perfume was crushed gorse and cinnamon. You could just catch it on the evening breeze.

In the pub we had another two brandies. Large ones. I think she was a little drunk. Flirtatious. I was drunker. My foot under the table met no resistance. When Rachel Fein came over and said hello, I asked her to join us. But she said, No, no, thank you. She didn't smile. She had to go home. Finish a book. Still in her dark winding sheet and her shawl.

"Finish a book! On Saturday night!" Donna snorted, after she'd gone. "The Lenau, God help us! Those who aren't mad are boring."

"Don't you like it there?" I asked, with the gently blurred solicitude of those in drink.

"Nobody *likes* it," she said, with sudden conviction. "You mustn't expect to like the place. But if you survive it, you'll have one of the most interesting minds around."

Home. Together. There seemed somehow to be no problem about it. Bill's bed was bigger, she said. When her makeup came off she was older. Years of spider lines around her eyes, some starting at the edges of her mouth. I didn't care. I kissed them. I changed my mind about breasts too—more geometry would make them less welcoming. Then my hands reached down.

"No," she said, a gentle whisper. "Not the full communion. But I'll make you happy anyway. Roll over on your back."

In the night once she murmured, "Tom, Tom," and I felt properly named at last. I kissed the lacquered blond mop of her hair.

In the morning she was gone.

It started to rain at twelve that Sunday and didn't stop. It was still raining the following morning when I set out for the Lenau. On the mat was a postcard. From Bill. Florence. It showed a picture of Michelangelo's *David*. On the other side was written:

> *Girls in their black scented stockings*
> *Girls in dark togs and a shawl*
> *All these are sweet*
> *But can hardly compete*
> *With big chaps who wear no togs at all*
> *See you Friday. The Archivist.*

9

Between the Black and White Spiders

So long as body presses upon body, how shall thought come to clarity? Exhaust yourself and then refuse yourself. All true work comes out of solitude and separation.
ALFRED DELAQUAY, *Diaries*

WHEN I ARRIVED AT THE INSTITUTE I WENT STRAIGHT TO THE library. Donna was sitting with a catalog open before her. I stood over her desk. She looked up finally and smiled vaguely.

"Can we meet?" I said.

"When's Bill coming back?"

"Friday."

"Maybe we'd best leave it for a while."

She saw the expression on my face. "Trust me," she said.

I found it hard to concentrate on the lecture that day. Lenski was droning on about Lenau's perceptions during his madness, how much of the world's art was there to defuse the primal terror, like dropping a portrait of your enemy in a coffin. Only at the end did I really register anything when he said, "Remember what Lenau taught us here. There is history and there is art, but there is no history of art. Each artwork offers us its unique criterion for its own evaluation. That much, at least, we can take on trust from Schelling and Novalis. All works are incommensurable, one with another. To try to string them out like beads on a necklace is to miss the point entirely. There are places where that is done. The Lenau is not one of them."

After the lecture I went back to the library. It was a different perfume I could smell as I leaned over to whisper to her. Juniper with thyme.

"I must see you."

She stood up expressionless and walked to the door. I followed her. In the corridor she suddenly showed me a face I'd never seen before.

"Don't ever do that again," she said, hard against the clench of her mouth. "What goes on outside is one thing. What goes on here is another. This is my *work*."

I went back home to Beaumont Street. I remembered something Grimshaw had once said to me, one bleak chill of a winter's day standing in front of one of his beloved ruins.

"Sometimes, Thomas Lynch, you have to choose between tears and anger. In my experience, anger is usually the better choice."

I went upstairs through the gallery and into Bill's room. I started going through the drawers systematically until I came to the ones with letters in. All in a jumble, sheets intermingled, from all over the world. Mostly from women. I could only find one from Donna. It was airmail from Oxford to him in Paris.

My dearest Bill,

You know the problem as well as I do. We don't own our feelings.

Yes, I do love you and yes I do still love him and no, I don't expect you to understand that.

I understand something about men. You must take your satisfaction where you find it. Perhaps in time this will change.

You don't have to rage so much, my darling.

Ever,

Donna.

Then I noticed the return address. *Donna Astley, 59 Walton Street, Oxford.* I put the letter back in its drawer and went down to my own room. I picked up *The Sustaining Wound.* Giles Astley. Her father? Published in 1907. The preface said it was in some ways "the work of a young man." How old was Donna? I flicked the pages. Started reading at random.

The potency of memory is inseparable from the damage it inflicts. The greatest memories hide themselves amidst the intricacies of more superficial rememberings. A memory of truly searing reality, which can neither be modified nor displaced, leads inevitably to madness.

One thing Lenski had said that day came back to me: Lenau's real imprisonment during his insanity was not in the asylum. It consisted of the walls of his memories and every image fastened on them, none of which he could curtain at any time. The maenads. The terrible murderous maenads, who broke the hearts and minds of their devotees.

I had not eaten and now wouldn't, but I had to get out. Into the air, into a pub. At the window of the Lamb and Flag I saw Rachel Fein at a table. I swerved away and kept walking.

■

It was only on Tuesday I realized that one of the two drawings I'd done was missing. I was sure I had left them together. Probably the least of my troubles.

Bill returned on Friday night and his smile soon pervaded the room. Five days before I'd hated him. Now I was glad he was back.

"What were you doing in Florence?"

"Delaquay was greatly devoted to the Uffizi and to some of the images in the Franciscan and Dominican churches."

As Bill said this he gave a great wink.

"And what are you devoted to, Bill?"

"I like those things too. And the Chianti. And the pasta."

"And the women?"

"Italians are closer to the earthly source of passion than the English. Even the tower at Pisa leans over, trying to get back down there."

He threw a packet of Italian cigarettes at me and we lit up.

"I've brought back some Chianti. Let's have some."

He started opening the bottle.

"Did Donna come round, by the way?"

I looked at him for a moment. I realized with some confusion that I wished she might be there now with both of us.

"Yes," I said. "She's in love with you, isn't she?"

"Not me, no. I was once in love with her, that's for sure. But she was in love with someone else, someone very close to me. And now you think you're in love with her. But I can't help thinking, Tom, son of my friend Tom, that you're trying to fill up a void too quickly. Maybe it's time you told the truth about your mother."

It's bad crying. For men anyway, it's always bad. Bill put his arm around my shoulder. Afterward we went and bought some fish and chips. Walking back, Bill brightened.

"You said you were interested in San Marco?"

"Yes, buildings as mnemonic structures, architecture as the framework of devotion."

"So go to Florence at Christmas. There are enough Delaquay funds to pay your way. Write one page on the gist of your research, and I'll submit it. You'll love Florence in the winter, believe me. And I can give you all the addresses you need for where to stay and where to eat. You don't really want to go back to the Yorkshire moors for the winter, do you?"

I didn't. So it was settled and I went. By that stage I avoided Donna's eyes whenever I went into the library, and she avoided mine. She didn't come to the apartments anymore, though Bill often stayed out overnight at weekends. He never said where he'd been. I thought it might be 59 Walton Street.

■

Rachel Fein was intrigued by my trip. When I told her it was probably inspired by the talk she had given about the different purposes of art, I could have sworn that her alabaster skin showed a brief tinge of red.

"You will write up your notes," she said. "When you come back we will have a session together discussing this. Your mind works, I've noticed that. Not all of them do. No matter. You must take Dante, of course. His vision of hell was so crucial in the formation of Lenau's thought. You know the famous fragment of his marginalia, Number 1007, I think? 'Between the Guelphs and the Ghibellines. The abyss. Poetry.'"

I asked Bill if there were a Delaquay *Inferno*.

"Of course," he said, "one of the classics."

He looked at me uneasily. "Not sending me up, are you? Did she tell you?"

"Did who tell me?"

"Donna. It's her copy. Well, technically it's her brother's. But she keeps it. Down at Walton Street. . . . Her brother Mervyn is a member. Donna's sort of crept in."

"Yes, I noticed."

He looked uneasy.

"Can you get it for me?"

"She'd probably exchange with the Milton for a while. I'm not even sure Mervyn's ever seen that. I'd have to say it was you, obviously."

"So say."

The day before I left, Bill brought me back the parcel.

"You shouldn't really be taking this to Florence, you know. It's against all the rules. If you lose or damage it, do me a favor and jump in the Arno. Bring me some wine back, they pay you enough."

I opened the package on the train. Another unseen Delaquay. I was more excited about that than seeing Florence. Inside Donna had put a little card. It was a copy of one of the images in the Institute's archive. A picture of a minor goddess kneeling to lay incense at an altar. On the back she had written:

> *Sorry I couldn't be her. Wanted from the start to be a certain woman in your life. Not my fault, believe me.*
> *Love, Donna.*

10

House of Memory

Rome. Florence. These great cities have engraved their
topography on the European soul. Even if they were razed to the
ground, you could look inside yourself and find those buildings.
ISAAC LENAU, *Marginalia*, 30

I AM STANDING IN SAN MARCO IN CELL NUMBER SEVEN. BEFORE me is Fra Angelico's *Mocking of Christ*. Between this and the *Crucifixion* in the chapter house I divide my obsessive's time. The *Mocking* shows Christ seated on a block, blindfolded and crowned with thorns. He holds a staff in his right hand and a ball in his left. These are the parodic accoutrements of his kingship. To one side a disembodied face raises its cap and blows a torrent of spit from its mouth into the Savior's face. Dis-embodied hands slap his cheek and beat the crown deeper into his bloodied scalp. He is draped in a white gown. The eyes, visible beneath the diaphanous blindfold, are closed. This king is more despised than the lowest soldier of the palace.

A moment later I stand before the crucifixion. The bad thief still curses the judgment laid upon him. But the good thief gazes into the face of the crucified Jesus. He receives his blessing with joy. He will be the first in Paradise that day, long before any of the saints.

Later in the café down the road I open up the Astley:

Memory was the most important of the five components of
rhetoric as far as the ancients were concerned. This is made plain
in the Ad Herennium, *for centuries ascribed to Tullius. There is a*

shift, though, by the time of the Middle Ages, when artificial
memory, the deliberate cultivation of remembrance, slides from
rhetoric toward ethics. This was perhaps inevitable for a culture
whose prime anamnesis was summed up by Boncimpagno: "We
must assiduously remember the invisible joys of paradise and the
eternal torments of hell." The illustrative material on the walls of
medieval cities (and Renaissance ones too) bears out this motif.
Wherever we turn we find emblems of the four last things—
death, judgment, heaven and hell—and every aspect of life, even
the meanest, points toward these inescapable realities.

I finished my coffee and started walking. I seemed to be doing a lot of
falling in love lately. Now I was in love with Florence. I walked across
the Piazza della Signoria and noted the spot where they torched
Savonarola and his Dominican companions to ashes. For falsely proph-
esying and so misleading the people of this city. Well, that's what they
said anyway.

In my bag I always kept the Astley and the Delaquay *Inferno.* I
wouldn't have dared to leave the Dante in my *pensione,* and I kept taking it out to look again at those illustrations. A great deal had been
burned into Delaquay's imagination in this topographic account of hell,
but there were two images I found inescapable. One was of Ugolino
starving to death in his cell as his own sons starved with him, and the
other was the she-wolf of lust in Canto One, who makes him give up all
hope of his ascent. To the wolf Delaquay had given the face of his succubus. And the figures in the cell were concentration-camp victims, staring madly at each other in the blindness of hunger. Delaquay published
his Dante in 1920.

It was my last day. I had been there for six weeks. I didn't really
want to go back, but lectures would start again next week at the Lenau.
That night I was on the overnight train to Paris.

I shared a sleeper with a Frenchman and his wife. They had been on
pilgrimage to see a young shop girl in a village outside Rome who had

seen an apparition of the Blessed Virgin. It must be true, the woman explained to me (for she spoke a little English), since the girl was far too stupid to have made it up. It heralded the end of the world, she explained. *"La fin du temps,"* she shouted at her husband, who was somewhat deaf. He nodded, his eyes wild with merriment at the prospect. He started to mutter to himself. I could make out very little, except for the odd word, *le feu, les volcans, les damnés.*

Finally, I let myself out into the corridor and watched the hills of Tuscany, looking exactly as they did in those paintings in the Uffizi, slide into darkness. Ugolino's children would be already dead by now, and he himself tumbling down through Dante's cosmogony. I looked back into the carriage from time to time but the French fellow had his *Sainte Bible* out and it looked to me as though he had his nose in the last part of it. His face was so radiant that I could only assume he was making a note of the volcanoes, the deluges, the great crescendo of miserable death. He was nosing out truffles in the Book of Revelation. I turned back to the dark rushing past me outside the glass.

Florence had almost tempted me back to orthodoxy. I thought I might even be able to live in San Marco myself, surrounded by the images of Christ's life and sacrifice. A whole building constructed to remind us that we must learn to forget ourselves entirely. Memory was the greatest of the five elements of rhetoric, but what was rhetoric itself? What was it for? To convert grammar into persuasion. To arrive at a conviction. The images of Florence spoke to me of Christ's voluntary annihilation at the hands of men he would not even damn as wicked. I started going to mass again and almost went up to take the eucharist. Almost.

It was odd, though, how much time I spent in that beautiful Renaissance city thinking of Ilkley. Staring into the Arno where it glides giddily into its rough water beneath the weir, I saw the Wharfe. All these different marks on stone. I remembered Grimshaw taking me to Baildon for the first time. Remembered his bony face staring at the stone urn in the local museum and turning on me.

"Baildon. The etymology has been construed as Hill of Baal. Wildly fanciful, they say. All the same, that urn you're looking at contained calcined bones, ashes, charcoal. It was discovered in an upright position two feet below the surface of the ground in the center of a circle of stones. The cremation of a youth, we must conclude. When the rest of them laugh, boy, pay attention. Why couldn't Joseph of Arimathea have come here to trade with Cornish tin-miners and preach the gospel? If you haven't sufficient credulity to believe that, well, you don't have enough to think the sun might still be shining tomorrow. Credulity is not our problem anymore. Incredulity is. The horrors shift before us, and we don't even credit them."

They climbed into their bunks finally, the two Gallic pilgrims, and I went back inside. There were mingled murmurs from above through the night. They weren't making love, though. I think they were saying the rosary in unison. French-style.

By the time I arrived back in Oxford Bill and Donna were married and Donna was pregnant, though not necessarily in that order.

11

The Marriage Feast
at Jericho

And when they wanted wine, the mother of Jesus saith unto him,
They have no wine. Jesus saith unto her, Woman, what have I to
do with thee? mine hour is not yet come. His mother saith unto
the servants, Whatsoever he saith unto you, do it.
JOHN 2:3–5

BILL'S ROOMS WERE UNNERVINGLY TIDY. THEN I REALIZED ALL
his things were gone. I saw the note on his table. On the envelope was
written: *For Tom Tomasovich. Open and change your life.* I opened it.

Dear Tom,
Didn't want to trouble you in sweet Firenze. Nor make you cut
short your trip.
    For administrative reasons beyond my control, a marriage
has been called for. One between myself and Donna. The miracle
of new life takes shape in her womb.
    I have moved into 59 Walton Street. The ceremony was dis-
creet. On Friday the fifth in the evening we shall have the some-
what belated reception.
    Come if you can. Come even if you can't.
    Bill.
P.S. Only really married to clarify a philosophical conundrum, but
don't tell Donna. Viz:

Bishop Berkeley addressed his girl, Flo:
Fix your beadies on this thing below
To assuage my deep fears
For it just disappears
When there's no one observing it grow.

Friday the fifth. Today. I sat down on Bill's big bed, holding the letter. Except it seemed it wasn't Bill's bed anymore.

By the time I arrived around seven the party had already gained its own momentum. There was a muffle of talk and laughter and a jingle of glasses and clouds of cigarette smoke. I wandered about carrying my little bag with the two bottles of Chianti in it. In the kitchen I saw Bill's head rising above the heads about him and stood there until he noticed me. That big smile opened up his face and he came over, bearing his full glass through it all like a chalice.

"Knew you'd make it," he said. "I told Donna, Don't worry, that Thomas boy will be here. And bearing gifts too." He peered into the bag. "Ah, Chianti. What a minister of grace you are."

He seemed, for the first time since I'd met him, truly sad. At the side of him appeared another man as tall as he was, but balding and unsmiling. Younger than Bill but aged by seriousness. Wearing an immaculate dark double-breasted suit and some sort of regimental tie. There was something in his face I felt I knew.

"Ah, Mervyn, good man," Bill said. "Let me introduce you to Tom Lynch the Second. Tom, this is Mervyn Astley, Donna's brother."

That was what I knew. The nose and eyes. I could see immediately that this was Donna's younger brother and I wondered again how old she must be.

"Ah, Tom, how do you do. I admire your work."

This confused me. Bill had already made off to open the Chianti.

"What work of mine have you seen?"

"Your wedding present for Donna and Bill is quite remarkable."

I shook my head slightly in my incomprehension. Mervyn took me by the elbow and guided me back into the front room, where he indicated with his glass toward the mantelpiece. Above it in a plain pine frame was my drawing of the tortured angel in *The Marriage of Heaven and Hell.* So that's where it went. It was the better of the two, that was without question.

"Whole evenings have been given over to the Milton," Mervyn was saying. "For some reason, it's one I'd never seen before. I trust the Dante has illuminated the depths for you. One day I'd like to see your other work, your own work, you obviously have a real talent. Drop in if you're ever in London."

He handed me a card from his inside pocket.

Mervyn Astley
Modern Paintings
Sculpture Engravings
Etchings Drawings
Illustrated Books
109 Cork Street
London W1

I was still looking at my own Delaquay when Donna came up to me.

"Thank you for our wedding present," she said. "It's the most beautiful one of all, and will be the most treasured."

It was about half an hour later that Bill laid an arm over my shoulder, and whispered, "Come out with your uncle for a pint."

We walked up to the pub.

"Just like old times," Bill said.

"Not quite."

"No," he said quietly. "No, not quite."

We sat in silence over our pints. Finally he spoke.

"It was a condition of the Delaquay Bequest that the Archivist be single. Delaquay was probably no fool in that regard, though Donna was furious last week when I told her. Anyway, there we are. My things are all gone, you probably noticed. Someone has to stand in as Archivist for a while. It's not an onerous job, as you've probably already realized if you've been monitoring old Bill at all. Almost all queries can be answered by reference to the Proceedings. Those that can't are referred to New York. There's nothing they can't answer. There are a lot of people who would like that job, Tom, a lot of Delaquay fanatics out there who'd probably shoot their wives to qualify.

"I wrote to New York and suggested you take over. I explained your youth, relative inexperience, the fact that you're at present an undergraduate at the Lenau. All that. I also said you're undoubtedly the most naturally gifted student of Delaquay I've ever met, or ever will. That drawing you gave to Donna . . . and by the way, thank you for what you wrote on the back. . . . You're smarter than I'd credited you with being, my boy. Maybe you could even bring some life into the organization before it dies, or falls apart in its squabbles."

"What are the squabbles, Bill?"

"There are those who say we must reproduce the work, that this whole business of refusing to allow the books, and more importantly the illustrations, to be printed in repro form will ultimately destroy us. The work leaks out, you see. Unofficial reproductions do appear, usually of a shoddy quality. Then the cry goes up somewhere, What's all the fuss about anyway? They have nothing worth hiding, which is the only reason they keep on hiding it. To hang on to their own mystique. The Masons of the visual arts, they call us. Little boys with secrets. Well, you and I know differently. If we ever allow it to be reproduced, it will defeat the whole purpose of Delaquay's vision."

"The depredations of lithography," I said.

"You've been reading the Proceedings?"

"No, it was something Grimshaw once said to me."

"Anyway, New York has agreed. To the astonishment of some, I can tell you. You'd have the whole place in Beaumont Street to yourself, and the Archivist's fees as well as your own stipend. You'd be set up, Tom. There's only one promise I would ask you to make. Don't let the Society go public. Every one of these books was held by Delaquay, turned over in his own fingers. Every illustration was produced by him by hand, even the etchings. He picked up the sheet and approved it, and signed it. When you pick one up—and you'll be picking up a lot from today— you're holding the hand of Delaquay. This is all that holds us together, this succession of hands and eyes. Break that and it's finished."

"I haven't even told you whether or not I want to do it."

"You want to do it," he said.

He was right too. As we walked back to Donna's house I remembered something.

"Remind me, would you, what it was precisely I wrote on the back of your wedding present."

"Don't tell me you've forgotten," he said, and laid his arm over my shoulder. "'Should auld acquaintance be forgot. There is an archivist you'd make a perfect wife for.' I didn't even realize you knew."

Back in the house I went upstairs to find the bathroom. As I came out, I saw a door open on the landing. I went in. It was Donna's bedroom. Well, now it was Bill and Donna's bedroom. Scents of all the lost perfumes over the years. On the chest of drawers were photographs in little shiny metal frames. Donna as a child. Donna and Mervyn playing on a swing. Donna at college. And there behind them all was a photograph of Donna with two men. One was a much younger Bill. And the other, the one she was kissing while Bill smiled and stared at the sky, was my father.

⑫

Rachel

And when the Lord saw that Leah was hated, he opened her womb: but Rachel was barren.

GENESIS 29:31

BILL'S BED WAS BIGGER. I SLEPT IN IT. DONNA HAD LEFT SOME memory of herself there, some inerasable trace of perfume, some shadow of a breast on a mattress. Now and then I tried to make love to the memory. Solitary ecstasies. Anyway, she was another man's wife now. And she'd once been that woman kissing my father, not that I'd ever known *him* except as a photograph, a legacy, and the big gaping hole he left in my mother. . . .

I had all the keys now. To all the doors and all the bookcases. There were mimeographed copies of those diaries from the 1890s. I started reading them.

May 1897. To Turandot off St. Germain. Found a beautiful little slut of no more than fifteen, but she'd probably already had as many men as I've had women. After making the necessary payments, I brought her back here. At first the ceremonies seemed to alarm her. I gave her more money though and she submitted. These techniques undoubtedly heighten sexual pleasure to a degree previously unthought-of. When the drugs had finally taken effect and she was unconscious I decorated her face with paints, and drew her at my leisure. This will be one of the illustrations for the Baudelaire: "Spleen."

One day an airmail letter arrived from New York.

Dear Tom,
Congratulations.
You are the youngest archivist the Society has had.
If you need anything, don't hesitate.

The Head Delaquay Archivist
New York City.

No name. A mysterious bunch. The thing I most wanted now was to lay my hands on a copy of Delaquay's Baudelaire. But there were other things to do. Like attend the Lenau.

Rachel Fein's lecture was entitled "Figures of Female Menace and Accusation." She ran through Aeschylus and the Furies, the Bacchae of Euripides, and the various shapings of Antigone, the truth-telling woman who menaces the state through blood loyalty. Cassandra, Grendel's mother, Eve in medieval art, Lady Macbeth. Then she surprised me by talking about Gerard Manley Hopkins.

"Among the more predictable female figures in Hopkins—the Virgin Mary, the young nun taking the veil, the grieving Margaret of 'Goldengrove'—there is one which reaches back in the clamor of its protest to the forceful prophetess of antiquity: the tall sister in 'The Wreck of the Deutschland.' This woman, exiled from Germany by persecution, calls out to God in the storm to save her. To save them all. He doesn't, of course, at least not in this life. We cannot read of her though, with her head through the skylight shouting out in her unsilenceable voice, without remembering Ulysses lashed to the mast as the sirens sing their heartbreaking song. *I* can never read it without thinking of Turner lashed to the mast so he could see the truth of the storm. Later he went back and painted that truth, but he sincerely believed at the time that he would die. Turner didn't die. The tall sister did."

Rachel Fein stepped from the dais. She came straight over to me.

"How did your work go in Florence?"

"It went well. Very well."

"You have something to show me?"

"Yes."

"We could discuss it this evening. Would you like to come to my flat?"

"Come to Beaumont Street," I said. "I have the place to myself now."

She nodded and walked out, throwing her shawl over her shoulder in a gesture which itself must have reached back to antiquity—that spring goddess throwing the seed as she treads the grass. It struck me that she hadn't asked for the number. It also struck me that I was already lonely in Beaumont Street.

I'd kept a bottle of the Chianti for myself and I bought some bread and cheese and olives in the market. No meat, I remembered that. I suppose I should have prepared the notes I'd taken in Italy (was this an evening tutorial?) but I had become so preoccupied with Delaquay's diaries that I found it hard to do anything but read them.

August, 1895. It is a Christian truism that God comes to you through the icons with which your own life is filled. It is the same with the devil. Our Lord Satan is equally curious about our daily preoccupations. The black sun of Gérard de Nerval's Les Chimères, the black and bottomless orbit of nothingness filled only with our wickedness. Last night's lascivious whore was weariness enfleshed. I suppose a sixteen-year-old boy might have thought her midriff jerks represented some kind of passion. I have walked too many streets. The odd shape of her mons though I sketched (for three extra francs). This will go into the Baudelaire.

My impatience to see Delaquay's Baudelaire was increasing. I was, I supposed, now in a position to make it possible.

Rachel arrived around six thirty. I offered to take her shawl—she declined. She must be six inches taller than I am. That girl the first day, what did she whisper to me? "Rachel Fein. Vegetarian. Never uses soap." She smelt different from Donna, but no worse. Intriguingly different. Like a field after it's cut. I poured her a glass of Chianti.

"How did you know which number, out of interest?"

"It's the Delaquay Society Oxford Archive," she said. "The Lenau once asked your Society to give us a talk, but our invitation was declined. You're a secret society, but everyone knows about you."

"I wouldn't have said secret society," I said.

"What would you have said?" I realized how large Rachel's brown eyes were. There was an unanswerable resonance to them when they stared at you unblinking.

"A little group that keeps itself to itself. A small, eccentric collection of bibliophiles."

"How sweet," she said, still not taking her eyes from my face. "Holding the one collection that won't let anyone else see it or reproduce its contents. Your Archivist has just married our assistant librarian. It's a small world."

"He's not our Archivist anymore," I said and I saw her face tighten with sudden curiosity. She unwrapped her shawl and walked over to the window. She turned around again and leaned back against the sill, sipping her wine.

"Why is Bill Blanchard no longer your Archivist?"

"Rules of the Society," I said. "You have to be single. Those are the terms of the bequest. Alfred Delaquay's requirements."

"Such quaint fellows. Who's the new one?"

"Me." I think I was aware that I was being indiscreet in the terms of my newly found post. I also realized that I was very pleased with myself.

"Must be something of an honor for someone at your age."

"Youngest in the history of the Society," I said and walked over with the bottle to refill her glass.

"One thing I've always wanted to know. How do you become a member of the Delaquay Society?"

"By accepting one of the books that Delaquay made, and all the terms attached to it."

■

It was to be another six months before I gave Rachel my Milton. On the night that we climbed into Bill's big bed I made her give me all the promises that Grimshaw had made me give him. Then I handed her the book. I'd still never made love to a woman, not in the full sense anyway. There was an angular and severe beauty about Rachel that had only gradually dawned on me, like light coming over the shoulder of that stone sphinx on Ilkley Moor. *She* had no objection to the full communion. As we pushed harder into each other I sensed, with one of those strange flashes of the speeding mind, this could have been Agatha's body forty years before.

"How do we make sure we won't have a baby?" I said, a little belatedly.

"You don't have to, my darling. That's the one thing I can't do."

In the morning when I woke up, Rachel was still sleeping. She had wrapped the sheets about herself exactly as she did the shawl. What an odd desert beauty. Her nose sliced out like a rock from the pale sands of her face. Her hair was chaos. I gently peeled back the sheets. Small breasts, large nipples. Her skin an unreal white all over. Only her haunches curved out from the flat thinness of her shape. By the time I came back up she was awake.

"Would you come to mass with me?" I said (it was Sunday morning). "I feel like giving thanks." Though I hadn't been for over six months.

She turned her head away in a sudden tug.

"No," she said. "No, I couldn't do that. Don't you know I'm Jewish?"

"You spoke highly of Hopkins all the same. It's my way of giving thanks."

"Then go by yourself," she said. "Go and give thanks by yourself. I spoke highly of the woman thrown out of Germany and how she had called on a Lord who didn't answer her. And how Hopkins had captured that. And her death. But I can't bear those ceremonies, those signs of the cross. The smell of incense makes me want to vomit. All Christianity I find alien, threatening. Roman Catholicism makes me ill."

I pulled her back to face me.

"Besides we have bread and wine here," she said, running her fingers down my spine. "And I'm body and blood enough. Don't you want what's here? Why do you have to go worship that dead Jew when you have a live one in your bed?"

Her thighs were bigger and stronger than mine.

"I don't know what I believe anyway," I said.

"Believe in me."

It took me a week to realize that every time I put a piece of soap on a sink it disappeared half an hour later. I learned to wash, as Rachel did, without it, rubbed myself with her salts and herbs. I too started to smell like mown hay.

"All flesh is grass," she said, unwinding her winding sheets and coming for me again.

13

Society's Child

*Women and books, and books and women. How many times I
sought oblivion, entering both.*
ALFRED DELAQUAY, *Diaries*

RACHEL'S LECTURE WAS ENTITLED "THE MACHINERY OF PATHOS."
I sat down there with the others as we watched her go up to the lectern,
swing her shawl back over her shoulder and start.

"The new age wakes to moving machinery. There are those, like the
Pre-Raphaelites, who would ignore that machinery and place wooden
mallets back in the hand and doves back in the dovecotes, but the age is
machine-tooled. The heroism of which Baudelaire spoke, which he said
was required of the artist in the city of modernity, is the heroism of sub-
jectivity moving through the order of the mechanical.

"Pathos, remember, is the effect of movement. Pathos is temporality
and waywardness contrasted with the idea of ethos. We might admire
the writhing serpents in the sculpture of Laocoön, and the agonistic
expressiveness to which they prompt the human body, but it is the stillness and composure, it is the *measure* of classical art which holds us in
its power.

"Such stillness has disappeared largely from the art of modernity,
except in its aspects of total abstraction and surrealism. When Lenau
first visited the John Soane Museum in London, he remarked that its
surreal beauty and seductiveness reminded him of nothing so much as
the large department stores of Paris. These fetishized objects, freed
entirely from the hands and tools and languages that created them, lived

outside time and pain, yielding themselves up to the purchasing eye. The Gothic stared manically across the room at classical serenity, Egyptian stone shrouds had to share the same floor with druidic sacrificial stones. The world's memories all brought under one roof. No connective thread but the dialectic thought of one eccentric architect, capable of turning the Bank of England into a temple of light, for whom the classical and the Gothic were merely alternating measures of the distance between earth and sun.

"The surrealist, in Lenau's view, had smashed the clock of history, exactly as those Jacobins shot at the clocks during the French Revolution. To set against the shadowless light of the Enlightenment, where it is always perfect noon, the surrealists opened the door into the dream. There time had been evacuated under the emergency regulations. There the objects of time are freed from all temporal use, thrown amongst the synchronous rejections that underlie all urban life. The *salon des refusés* is the gallery of all genuinely modern art.

"This could be put another way: the classical measure has shifted to the realm of the machine, and the machine is nothing but movement, for a machine in repose is essentially dead. The iconic epitome of this characteristic of modernity is Duchamp's famous *Nude Descending a Staircase No. 2* of 1912. Here the human body has simply been replaced by a machine, a machine of cubist proportion and perspective, a machine which moves brightly and reflectively through the dark that surrounds it.

"This is in its way dispassionate. By the time we reach the Fascist fetishism of Marinetti, the machine is no longer standing in (as a sort of metonymy) for the body, it is now entirely superior to it. The body must worship before it and in it. The body must accept its subjugation and applaud as it is crushed or blown to pieces by iron and steel in the glorious machinery of war.

"In the Communist kitsch of the Stalin dictatorship, the torsos of workers increasingly approximate to machines. The ideal Stakhanovite body is in fact entirely mechanical, incapable of hunger or thirst, never tiring, and requiring no sexual solace. Between the Fascistic and Communistic arts, there is an analogous move toward the relentless tranquillity of the machine. The pathos of modernity is operated by a switch.

"Switch now to Rembrandt. In all the faces of Christ he painted the pathos has been turned inward. There is a species of classical tranquillity about these portrayals, even though in many respects Rembrandt was the least classical of artists. But the pathos of suffering, and the passion, which is literally a suffering shared, is held in stillness. Even in the self-portraits the ravages of time have left their signature in the flesh of the artist and then themselves left the frame. And we are left with the composure, the trace after the asymmetry of temporality has done its worst. There are moments of radical movement in Rembrandt's self-portraits, for example the *Self-portrait as Zeuxis.* There all the movement is in the eyes and the mouth. It is the movement of laughter, as the only defensive maneuver against time.

"Landscape, it is true, offered its temptations. Landscape for a time became emblematic of violence of mood, expressed through the ceaseless motion which is nature. But at the very edge of visual modernity we have Cézanne, who effectively rediscovered the Pythagorean mysticism of geometry. As surely as Piero della Francesca, Cézanne finds in nature a hymn to the perfection of the five perfect shapes. The chance, the *hasard,* of his cardplayers, is offset already by the shapes to which they can be decomposed.

"The most violently subjective art the world has ever produced is matched consistently in our time by the mechanicist menace of determinism. In this sense there is no boundary between aesthetics and politics. We have made our shapes and cries as formulaic as those of the machines that tend us. Even the formulae of our improvisations observe this symmetry. The pained breath of Charlie Parker emits its cries, in the elaborate unstillness of the bebop world, through the steel machinery of a saxophone. Piet Mondrian makes exquisite abstract mantras from the fleeing yellow of the New York cabs beneath his Manhattan studio.

Jackson Pollock discovers a lacemaker's symmetry in the blood soon to dribble from his own crushed skull.

"All our creations must now pass through machines. Whether it is the words of the book or the image of the artist, or the frames of the director, for we live in the age of repetitive reproduction. I would direct you again to the title of Duchamp's painting: *Nude Descending a Staircase No. 2.* The primacy of authenticity has been lost forever. By the time we see it, what we see is secondary.

"The body has become inseparable from the machine. Even the voice, that guarantor of our real presence, can never sound the same again to the ear which has heard the perfection of recorded voices. Once again Baudelaire is remarkable in his early grasp of the dimensions of modernity: Paradise, he said, is artificial."

■

Rachel was a skeptic.

"All this secrecy. All these whispered rules. Anonymous archivists in New York. This is *verboten* and that is *verboten.* We live in the age of mechanical reproduction. With these books, it's as though there's still a medieval scriptoire with hands illuminating unique copies of gospels. A stranger comes up the mountain once a year and you decide whether or not to show him anything."

"It's only because it is the age of mechanical reproduction that it means anything at all," I said. I'd read all the Proceedings at least once. By now I'd seen Delaquay's *Anatomy of Melancholy,* his *Les Chimères,* his Hölderlin *Patmos,* and his *Alice in Wonderland.* And I had done my own drawings of every illustration in these books.

"Two things happened that brought all this about," I said. "Delaquay knew Doré and he saw what the engravers and the printers between them did to his work. The bad cutting, the bad inking, and the shoddy papers—his work was almost unrecognizable by the time it appeared. It was, in one sense, no longer *his* work. Delaquay witnessed all this with quiet disbelief.

"Then one day he held in his hands a book of hours. Fourteenth-century French. That was the turning point of his life. He understood that this book could not be reproduced. That was a lying word. A dim, distant, coarsely colored copy could be run off the machines. That's not reproduction, is it, if one thinks of what that word means? The book of hours had never separated hand from eye. A tradition of hands and eyes held it together. That was the tradition which photography and lithography and film between them abolished. Delaquay said it could be restored, but only with a handful of people. Its restoration was dependent on it not being universalized, though universalism in other respects was the condition of our lives. What you go through does not leave you unaffected. The machines the work has to go through to be made available leave their signatures upon it. In a sense they dictate what the work ends up being. Those Lambeth prophecies of Blake—the fact that he was not setting up a text in movable type but engraving the words themselves directly onto metal, just like the illustrations, this is what gives the work its distinction."

"Blake was a jobbing engraver, he had to make a living. If Delaquay had had to make a living . . ."

"Then there would be no Delaquay Society," I said. "And you and I wouldn't be here. He described himself as a useless man, of no use to the age. His private money freed him from the age."

Rachel shook her head into a storm of hair. She couldn't escape it, though. I kept finding her turning the pages of the Milton. More and more often she looked at that book. Delaquay was seeping through the skin of her fingers. She was fascinated by the succession of shrivelings and degradations which Delaquay portrayed Satan undergoing in the first two books of the poem.

"It's real," she said, her head coming up suddenly off the page, "he's captured something real. There are borrowings from Dürer's iconography, but there is a reality about this and I can't work out where it comes from."

"His life," I said. I went and found the extracts from his diaries and gave them to her. She sat for two hours and read about his activities in the 1890s, all the devotees of evil, all the little rituals he practiced. I heard her slam the book shut.

"I don't like this," she said. "I've never believed all this mumbo jumbo."

"Hocus-pocus would be more exact," I said. *"Hoc est corpus."*

"I know what evil is," she said. "I've seen evil in the streets. It has a man's shape."

"Delaquay was a man. You wouldn't be getting upset if you didn't believe it. What he talks about, it's true. You know it the same as I do. I don't understand it either, but that's not a game he's playing there."

"We had angels," she said quietly, as though talking to herself. "Even some demons. Asmodeus we made and gave to you. The Babylonians made us a gift of their underworld—we did spend some time with them at their invitation—and we made Gehenna out of that. A dark prince named Arsiel, the black sun. But it's your lot who created hell, so fascinated with every inch of it. There's a Talmudic injunction which says one may not dwell on the afterlife, whatever it should bring. This is not why we are placed on earth. No Jew could have written the *Inferno.* Not until this century anyway. Now we don't need to imagine it—we can photograph it."

"We can write theses too," I said. "Mine's 'The topography of hell: Europe's dark dream,' remember." Rachel was as intrigued by the subject as I was.

"People's versions of hell always correspond to what they see around them," she said. "Each hell is just their own world with the mercy taken out. Brueghel's *The Triumph of Death,* even Bosch's hallucinations—people tormented by the implements of their time. Piranesi's *Carceri* represent a quite constructible hell. Look at Doré's drawings in *London* and it's been put up. Within a hundred years, Piranesi's version of hell has been built along the Thames. His opium den is surely a scene from the *Inferno,* drawn directly from life. His Quixote is an inmate of the world's Bedlam."

"What do you really believe, Rachel?"

She fell silent for a few moments.

"That it is better to kiss flesh than tear it. Better to feed children than shoot or gas them. I believe in the tormented. I believe in your Jesus, another tormented Jew, tortured to death by the policemen of his day. Different uniforms, the same job. I'm not sure what you've all managed to turn him into. You seem so ready to forget that he was a Jew killed by Romans, you Roman Catholics."

"Delaquay was tormented," I said, putting my hand on her arm. Such thin arms. Bones held together with blue veins.

"Yes, that's why what he did was real. But if his demons came from hell, it was from the hell inside him. You remember what Blake said about Dante: his *Inferno* was real not *despite* but *because* it was imagined."

Often now I didn't go to the Lenau. After the initial energy of the first course of lectures there was a leveling down. Everything they had to teach they could do largely in three months. After that it was for people to apply the method using their own intelligence. I went to the library, I worked my way through the annotations and marginalia. I had Rachel with me at home anyway. She lectured me half the time as it was. Lenski's talks I never attended. Now and then we would pass in the corridor. He didn't acknowledge me.

I had found a small photograph of Delaquay in one of the drawers. I had it put into a silver frame I bought and it sat on my desk. He was pale and bearded. Out of his ravaged face the eyes blazed. Above him was an enormous crucifix fastened to his wall. This was the time toward the end. There were no physical descriptions I could find but he looked to me like a small man.

I was often working away at my versions of his drawings when Rachel came back. Sometimes I dispensed with the original altogether and worked blind. Delaquay's style had now become indistinguishable from my own. That was how I drew. Rachel didn't like it. She would look over my shoulder.

"You spend too much time doing those things. The whole point of copying is to absorb the lessons of masters and move on into your own work."

"This is my own work," I said. "This is the only work I have."

"Is this the real reproduction, then?"

"I don't know," I said, "but there's nothing mechanical about it."

One day there was a knock at the door. Rachel was at the Institute. I looked out of the window onto Beaumont Street and saw a man of about fifty, who looked profoundly uncomfortable. He was peering about him nervously through his thick glasses as though he thought someone might be following him.

He was Dr. Stephen Goodridge from Gloucestershire. He wished to see the Archivist. He was shocked to hear that I was now in that eminent position.

"But where's Mr. Blanchard?"

"He married," I said.

The man looked so ill at ease that I suggested a drink. He nodded and I poured us both a whiskey.

"What's the problem exactly?" I said.

He opened his briefcase and took out a little brown bag which obviously contained a book.

"You must understand," he said, "that were this not a case of necessity, I wouldn't be here. But it is. Open it."

It was the Delaquay Baudelaire.

"I must part with it," he said.

"You wish to exchange it," I started, wondering where Rachel had put the Milton I had given her.

"No, I do not," he said with sudden vehemence. "And I won't. I'm afraid, whatever the rules say, I intend to sell this book. And if the Society won't buy it back from me, then I know a gentleman in London who will. I thought at least you deserved the first offer."

I knew that such a sale would break the fundamental rule of the Society, but I was already turning the pages. I had waited a long time for this.

"How much would you intend to sell it for?"

"One thousand pounds. I'll not take less. The gentleman in London has made it clear . . . never mind. One thousand, I'm afraid, or I will go elsewhere."

I left him with a copy of the Proceedings in his hand and went straight to the bank. There were currently eleven hundred and twenty-four pounds in the account, the teller informed me. When I came back I sat down and wrote out a check for the amount.

"How do I know that it won't—"

"Delaquay Society checks don't bounce," I said. "But if you would like to contact the manager of the branch to reassure yourself . . ."

"There'll be no need," he said. He stood up to leave. He appeared to be shaking.

"Be careful who you give that to," he said. "Flowers of evil. Dark little blossoms."

He was gone. It sat there on the table. I poured myself another whiskey and walked around it a few times. This was the major work of those bad times. This was the clinching evidence of the Dark Theorists. *Les Fleurs du mal.* It had taken him five years. I went and pulled out the relevant volume of the Proceedings:

> *At first this great work contaminated me. Then in time it was I who came to contaminate the book. We shared our disease—the disease of our time—so freely that we created a new book entirely from the joint infection. Baudelaire attempted to capture every vice in Paris. The ones he left out I have included for him. If the age could only see itself in these words, these engravings, it would understand at last that its soul is dead.*

I opened the book. By the time I had turned the last page the first part of my life had finished.

When Rachel came back that afternoon, I was already drawing. The infection had penetrated me too. I had simply never seen anything like this. She stood behind my shoulder.

"No," she said. "No, don't do that."

"It's *Les Fleurs du mal,*" I said, holding up the book. "I've got it."

"That's sick," she said. "If he had to do that, then he's already falling in my mind. But you, you shouldn't be doing that. Treat it as a matter of scholarship if you have to, write your own essay on the Dark Theory, but don't follow him."

I was already drawing again by the time she had finished her sentence.

■

I didn't want Rachel to leave and I told her that.

"It's either me or that book," she said.

She moved out the next Sunday.

When Bill called round I'd not washed or changed for a few days. I hadn't eaten much either. I did go out from time to time to buy another bottle of Scotch and some cigarettes. I'd done fifty drawings. They were the best, I knew that. Bill looked at them carefully.

"Remarkable," he said evenly. "Had a note from the bank manager about an extraordinary payment, by the way. One thousand pounds. Almost emptied the account. Made payable to Stephen Goodridge who, if I recall, used to own that book on the table."

I'd started drawing again as he spoke. It was a discourtesy I was sure Bill would understand. I couldn't stop producing these marks on the paper.

"I had no choice," I said. "He would have sold it in London otherwise."

"I'm surprised you didn't try to consult anyone else," Bill said.

"Help yourself to the whiskey," I said. We were both already smoking. Cigarettes no longer made me feel sick—my body had acclimatized to that poison.

"You shouldn't have done it, you know."

"He'd have wanted it," I said.

"Who would?"

"Who do you think?" I said. "Delaquay."

"So you know what he'd have wanted now, do you?"

"Better than anyone else does. To be honest, Bill, I think what he'd probably want now is for you to leave and let me get on with this."

Bill turned around with his hand on the door.

"Donna had a baby boy this morning. Eight pounds, two ounces. We're calling him Tom. We wanted to know if you would be a godfather."

14

Expulsion

They looking back, all th'Eastern side beheld
Of Paradise, so late thir happie seat . . .
JOHN MILTON, *Paradise Lost*

DELAQUAY HAD NO CHILDREN. FOR HIM AS FOR BAUDELAIRE THE idea of marriage and procreation is somehow laughably inappropriate. One thing became clear within days of immersing myself in the Baudelaire—this world was a lot closer to Grimshaw than it was to Blake. This wasn't a universe in which the unfettered imagination drove all before it with magisterial antinomian laughter. Every desire awaited its defeat, every hope its contradiction, every ecstasy its hangover. Here the imagination lived in a dark shadow of the condemned world, a shadow called ennui and spleen. Only the defeated were even worthy of regard.

There were a number of poems I kept coming back to over and over. One was "Spleen" itself:

> *Like the emperor of endless rainy plains*
> *Impotently rich, cradled in antique loins*
> *Disgusted at the Court Instructor's smile*
> *Bored with hounds, tarantulas, the gleeman's tale;*
> *Nothing pays the mortgage of his frown, not a falcon*
> *Murderously feathering the sky nor treason*
> *Delivering its flagellants outside for public slaughter.*

Even the jester half-wit taunting to gross laughter
Leaves his lips uncurved. His bed, bejeweled
With insignia and heraldry, leaves him cold
As do the ladies waiting on his court, for whom
Each crowned head tops Adonis. Spreadeagled in his tomb
They can make nothing come, not one moony circus smile
As he shoots-up like it was going out of style.
Alchemists who turn their urine into squirts of gold
Can't straighten out the crease on which their pages fold.
The Romans cut their veins in baths of tepid water
(And brothel-keepers always banish the word "later").
Who can re-heat this phthisic body in a black silk hood
     Veins green-sliming doped oblivion, not blood?

The figure of sensual decrepitude which Delaquay had engraved to match this was horrifying in its self-awareness. If it was consumed by anything it was a paralysis of self-knowledge. The tarantula's hypodermic cutting into the veins made no impression. The lasciviously decorated women, offering him their breasts, didn't even catch his eye. This was the king of boredom, sated with every stimulant the world affords. The face was Delaquay's.

The other poem was "Le Gouffre":

His abyss hissing always at his side
Pascal's heart wagered at the edge of things
Where the blade (in judgment over nothing) swings—
A metronome of progress that has died

Height, depth, a ubiquity of parched
Insistent silence, space's manic stare
Beguiles the void that's stalling everywhere
To blazing eyes the hypnotist has torched

And I fear sleep like the minutest rip
That opens to a roaring gap
Turning inside-out the universal

Each windowpane my fingertip touches
Rattling as the finite unlatches
To endless horror, vertigo and time's reversal

Again Delaquay had portrayed himself, staring into the vast glazed expanse of the world, and being given back only the image of his exhausted self. His own eyes were the hypnotist's, but they were not powerful enough to put himself into the trance he craved.

In one of his diary entries, Delaquay had written:

Baudelaire. Time merely the motion of condemnation. The revolution of 1848 a parody of hope. Drugs, drink: the annihilation of anxiety. The world a heap of allegorical dead shapes. The mind of man hovers over this like the Spirit hovering over chaos, but in this pantomime Genesis nothing takes shape from the chaos but these poisoned elegies.

I looked at the prancing whores again. He had managed to convey somehow that one could only want these creatures mechanically. Real desire would not go near them. Rachel!

I took the Baudelaire with me wherever I went. It was in the pocket of my coat in the church when I promised to renounce Satan and all his works and pomps over the head of young Tom as they held him by the font. I was badly hung over but he looked pretty ugly to me, having dispensed with the finer features of either his father or his mother.

The reception was given at the house of a friend of Donna. I took the white wine and refused the sandwiches. The baby was being carried around for people to murmur at in admiration. Bill was explaining to a couple of people why he had left it so late to start a family. "I thought I might be better suited in the twilight of my years," he said. "The owl of wisdom flies at twilight, you know."

"Is that so?" the woman said.

"Hegel," the man said.

Bill was smiling again.

> *"Hegel cooed to a somewhat hirsute*
> *Prussian Mädchen in spiked hat and boot*
> *You're this thinker's highlight*
> *Little owl-eyes at twilight*
> *Minerva, my cute Absolute."*

"Oh, very good, Bill. Very droll," the man said.

Come back to me, Bill, I thought, you're wasted on these characters. I made off to the kitchen to find a full glass. Donna was there. She gave me a skeptical look. In the background, on the gramophone, the breathy trumpet of Chet Baker meandered its melancholy way about a tune.

"Rachel Fein may come," she said. "I invited her, along with other . . . people at the Lenau."

"That's nice, Donna," I said. I hadn't realized until this moment how profoundly I disliked her.

"Well, congratulations," I said. "Another Tom."

I could have sworn Bill was avoiding me. A lady in a tiara (at least I think that's what it was—didn't see many of those in Ilkley) had decided to be charming to me.

"And what do you do?" she said, her voice wrapped in the silk of inherited wealth. "Are you a student at the Lenau?"

"Actually, I'm the Archivist of the Delaquay Society," I said.

"Oh, really. What's that?"

"I can't tell you if you don't already know," I said. "I'm afraid it's a secret."

I decided I'd had enough of this. I had renounced evil on behalf of my miniature namesake and now I wanted to be back in my own rooms with my Baudelaire and my whiskey, to gaze at evil unrenounced. Bill saw me making off to the hall. Suddenly he scurried over. "Where are you going, Tom?"

"Home," I said. "I think Grimshaw's dislike of polite society must have rubbed off."

"Come on," he said, pulling the coat off my shoulders. "Come and have another drink."

We sat in the conservatory and stared out at the rain. It had been raining for four days and all the infections trapped in Oxford's stones had been released into the air.

"I suppose I'm in trouble," I said.

"There are concerns about you," he said, without looking at me. "To be honest, Tom, there's a general feeling that you were placed in a position of responsibility before you were ready for it. I blame myself here. It was my idea. I just didn't expect you to change quite so much so quickly."

"Have I changed?" I said.

"My dear fellow, even you must have noticed, surely. A year ago you were a gauche but likable young man down from the wild moors of Yorkshire and finding your way about. Now you're drunk all the time, locked up with your book—a book you offended everyone in the Delaquay Society by illegally buying out of the Society's funds. As if that weren't enough, you're having an affair with a Jewish divorcée."

"Divorcée?"

"You'll have to learn to do more homework on your women, Tom. Until two years ago Dr. Rachel Fein was better known as Dr. Rachel Lenski. I shouldn't think you've helped your prospects at the Lenau there at all, frankly."

I stood up and put my glass on the table.

"I'm going, Bill."

"You can come to us," he said, and again looked away from me.

"I don't need to come to you," I said.

"Remember. You can come to us. We both want you to."

I reached Beaumont Street soaked through with the rain and I put my key in the door. It wouldn't turn. I examined it to make sure it wasn't bent. It was as straight as ever but it wouldn't turn in the lock and the lock felt different. Then I saw the envelope tucked into the doorjamb. It was airmail. I stood there in the rain as the blue ink streaked across the paper and read.

> *Dear Tom,*
>
> *It is with great sadness that I have heard of your behavior.*
> *What you have done would be intolerable from any member.*
> *From the Archivist of the Society, it is difficult to think of a suitable response.*
> *You are relieved of your duties as of now.*
> *Fifty pounds will be paid to you from the account to help you reorganize your life.*
> *Yours,*
> *The New York Archivist.*

On the back of the envelope, in a different hand, was written: "Your belongings are at the Blanchards'."

The miscellaneous chimes of Oxford told me that the pubs had opened. With Baudelaire in my left pocket and my letter of dismissal in my right, I made my way to the Lamb and Flag.

I was on my second large whiskey when Rachel came over and sat down at the table. I hadn't seen her—I was turning the pages of the book.

"Still reading, I see."

"Yes," I said, "nothing much else to do now."

"How's that?" she said.

"I'm no longer the Archivist of the Delaquay Society and since I no longer have keys to the rooms there, I take it my allowance from them has ceased too."

"What did you do?" she said.

"I sinned. *Mea culpa, mea culpa, mea maxima culpa.*"

"You can only explain it in Latin, can you?"

"I bought this Baudelaire. I introduced filthy folding money to the asylum of the Delaquay. I have been punished."

"Where will you stay?"

"My things have been deposited at the Blanchards', so I'll perhaps stay there for a day or two."

"Oh, don't stay with that blond tart," she said, and took hold of my hand. "Come and stay with me, if you like."

"Be frightened I might bump into your husband," I said. "You never know when he might drop by, Dr. Lenski."

Rachel let go of my hand and finished her drink.

"You understand nothing, do you? So self-preoccupied you understand nothing at all."

"You might have told me."

"You never asked. Anyway it wasn't important. What you do, Tom, there's no love in it, the way you thump away. I thought I might be able to find where it was inside you, in time. That room locked at the back of your head. That's what you need the key for. You won't find it in a bottle, Tom. They put ships in there but no keys. Ships and little babies with pickled faces."

As she left I nearly ran after her, nearly asked if I could go back with her after all. Nearly.

Bill answered the door.

"Come in, my lad, you're soaking."

I could hear Donna in the other room soothing the baby.

"All your things are here," Bill said. "Up in the spare room. You'll stay for a while?"

"I've nowhere else to go, Bill. When did you know?"

He looked uneasy. "Yesterday. They told me yesterday."

"And you told them I'd be at your baby's christening this morning."

"Have a drink, Tom."

"Just this once I don't think so, Bill, if it's all the same. I'll go lie down for a while."

I suppose they didn't realize how their voices carried in that house, particularly when they were cross, but I could hear most of the conversation from upstairs.

"He's not staying here, Bill, I don't care what arrangements you make. I've just had our baby. I don't want him drinking himself stupid here and mooning about."

"Where can he go? He doesn't even have any money to attend the Lenau anymore. The tutorial fees came from the Society."

"He never goes anyway. Stopped after he took up with that Jewish bitch."

"He'll have to get a job. Or go back to live with Grimshaw."

"I'll talk to Mervyn in the morning," she said. "He might have some sort of idea. He liked him when he met him. You'll have to get him sobered up, though, Bill. He looks as though he's just climbed off the refugee boat."

That night I slipped out of the house. I went back to the Lamb and Flag. Now I really wished I'd gone with Rachel. I hoped she might come. She didn't. On the way back to Donna's house I saw the light on in the Delaquay rooms and stood at the other side of Beaumont Street in a doorway. After a few moments I saw Grimshaw, arguing furiously with someone, his arms motioning up and down. I started to cross the road, then I remembered what I'd done. I stopped, looked up, and saw the man he was arguing with appear. A younger man. Probably about Bill's age.

15

Cork Street

Every soul is its own secret society.
ALFRED DELAQUAY, *Diaries*

SO IT WAS THAT I CAME TO WORK FOR MERVYN ASTLEY. BILL
took me down on the train. At the station, we went into a bar. Bill bought
himself a whiskey and me a lemonade.

"You're turning up for your new job sober," he said. "Best learn to
stay that way too."

The way he smiled at this remark made me cross. But then everything made me cross now. When I wasn't drunk I was hung over. Either
way, I was cross.

"I'll have a whiskey," I said to the barman. "A large one. You can
put it in that lemonade."

"You're going to have to change your ways," Bill said, smiling again.
"If you'd only kept your nose clean at the Delaquay . . ."

"Out of interest, Bill," I said, "was it you or your wife who used to
sleep with my old man?"

That took the smile from his face. I thought for a moment he was
going to cry.

"Here's your fifty pounds," he said, reaching into his pocket. "And
this parcel which Rachel Fein dropped round for you. Stay away for a
nice long while, will you?"

"With pleasure. Who's going to be the Archivist of the Delaquay
now, Bill?"

"They've modified the rules," he said hurriedly. "Allowed me to work there part-time."

"I'm sure the money will come in handy, eh? Not to mention the use of the premises should married life ever . . ."

He was gone. Rachel had said I could love no one, and maybe she was right. I'd made all these people hate me and I really had no idea why. Not a single one of my actions or words had been premeditated. That's simply the way it happened on the day. I opened the parcel from Rachel. In it was the Delaquay *Paradise Lost.*

Mervyn Astley. They said he'd been in the Household Cavalry once, but had left in murky circumstances and it didn't do to ask him about them. Certainly he had a way with him that suggested some kind of military training. This only applied to his backbone, however. In every other respect he was seriously bent.

In the first month he taught me how to distinguish genuine from fake items. It was usually simple enough, employing about five basic techniques. We separated the authentic from the inauthentic between us. But they all went into the showroom at about the same price anyway.

"You must understand," he said to me, "most of the people who come here are moderately to excessively wealthy, and extremely stupid. I have come to the conclusion that in England there seems to be an inherent incompatibility between inherited wealth and intelligence. These people would once have employed someone with a modicum of competence to go and buy their pictures and books for them. Me, for example. But no longer. They wish to demonstrate their own savvy about matters artistic. I always compliment them on their taste and discernment and so must you, Tom. That's what they want to hear, that every single one of them could have been another Berenson. Then get the check signed."

I think it must be something to do with my early years but when I leave a place, it becomes unreal along with the people in it. All the color drains away. The tastes, the smells. The touch of flesh. Rachel, Bill, Donna. All gone as I enthused about the latest Modigliani to hang on the walls of the Astley Modern Gallery, Cork Street. Whether Modigliani's own hand had ever touched it or his eye ever seen it, didn't halt the flow of my informative and tactful talk. I have always been a quick learner. I soon picked up the patter and it was, after all, a subject in which I had a genuine interest. To be fair, I had been noted as a possible future lecturer at the Lenau. Once upon a time I'd been the Archivist of the Delaquay Society too.

That Christmas I received a card from Grimshaw:

Congratulations on your appointment as shop salesman.
Hope the commissions are good.
   You may write from time to time, you know, or even come to see us, should things grow really desperate.
   Take care of yourself.
   Love from Patrick and Agatha.

Shop salesman! Though as usual with Grimshaw, when one thought for a moment about what he was saying, he had a point.

■

I had a pleasant enough flat in Paddington. I had my Delaquays. I couldn't drink during the day at the gallery but I often got drunk at night. And once a month I went to find a whore in Soho.

I'd come to the conclusion that the two keys to Baudelaire's world were intoxication and prostitution. These were the two ways in which you could make the movements of the human mind and body as mechanical as the movement of the stars, and thus escape momentarily from the great ash heap of reality. If I could have afforded it, I'd have gone to Soho every night.

I would drink first in the Coach and Horses and then, late in the evening, set out on my journey. It was the journey which I think afforded the most pleasure. For that hour London dissolved into doorways opening their mouths to show glittering women who smiled at your money. I liked the pure ritual of it. This was true understanding. They knew what you wanted and you knew what they wanted. And after you come, you go. A seesaw symmetry about it. They were usually older than I was. One of them even called me "the little man."

As I walked back in the early hours I often remembered Blake's lines in *Jerusalem:* "Is that Mild Zion's hill's most ancient promontory, near mournful Ever-weeping Paddington?" It did seem to rain a lot. It struck me that Roman Catholics have a natural aptitude for vice: our theology prepares us for it. Most of the other brands of Christianity seem to deviate so easily into optimism. In the Delaquay Baudelaire, next to the poem about Icarus, there was a drawing of a figure falling from the sky with wings ablaze. It had taken me some time to realize that the wings were identical to those of Saint Michael in *Paradise Lost.* So much for human aspiration. Angels fly. We fall.

16

Delaquay Again

C'est l'exécution du catéchisme.
ARTHUR RIMBAUD, *Une Saison en enfer*

THE PROBLEM WAS MONEY.

Mervyn's Jaguar was parked outside the gallery. We were both looking at it as we waited for the rain to come. And I think we both noticed at about the same time.

"My God," Mervyn said, "my car. Look at the bloody thing. It looks too old."

"Or not old enough," I said.

"The paintwork. The tires."

"You're not cutting the figure you once did, I'll tell you that for nothing."

Trouble was, most of Mervyn's art was now the real thing and the margin wasn't large enough to keep the gallery going much longer. There was a fine Matisse, a seductive Modigliani, an early Moore, books with illustrations by Picasso. But no one was buying them. People sometimes looked at them, as Mervyn praised them for their taste, but they didn't buy. And my wages hadn't moved for four years. I didn't have a car at all. The clapped-out Jaguar would have suited me fine.

The next day Mervyn left his Delaquay Dante on the table. I kept turning the pages and remembering Florence. San Marco. Fra Angelico. And after I had come back to England, Rachel. Europe's dark dream. The topography of hell. I regret little, it's not my way, but I came close to some regrets that day. I could still smell Rachel's flesh. And the next day

I brought the Baudelaire and the Milton from my flat and put them on the table too. We said nothing all day. Nobody came into the gallery. At five o'clock Mervyn turned the sign to closed, and went back to his office. He emerged with a bottle of whiskey.

"Your drink as I remember?" he said.

"One of them, certainly."

I'd come to the conclusion about Mervyn that, bright and well informed as he was, he simply had no interest in his fellow man. He would talk spiritedly to a potential customer but then afterward sink into morose silence. Now and then a leggy young woman would climb out of his car, displaying all the grace and self-possession of the deportment school as she did so, but they never lasted long, these women. I would imagine the strain of having to talk to them even intermittently proved too much for Mervyn to bear. He did come alive, though, on the subject of money.

"Are you planning on selling the Delaquay books?" I asked finally.

"Good God, no," he said. "That would be suicidal."

"Then what?"

"Your pay's not excessive, is it, Tom?"

"I only labor for the muses, as you know, Mervyn, but I think it fair to say that I'm employed by a skinflint who'd give Ebenezer Scrooge a good run for his money."

It was impossible to wound Mervyn; he took accusations of meanness as a compliment to his business acumen.

"How much would you like?"

"Just more, Mervyn, a lot more."

"So would I. Still have those drawings you did?"

"Yes."

"Bring them tomorrow."

I gave them to him the next day. He spent an hour at the table looking through them, backward and forward. Not a word. Then finally:

"They grow stronger as they go on," he said. "A little freer all the time. How much do you know about Delaquay?"

"Probably as much as anyone else does," I said.

"You know which books he illustrated?"

"I know which books he's known to have illustrated. According to Grimshaw, who did actually meet him, he was shrouded in mystery. No one knew anything for certain."

"But you could give me a list of the books the Society reckoned he'd illustrated?"

"I could."

"Then write it out for me today. Here in the gallery. I'll take it home with me tonight. I need to think. I'll keep these drawings of yours in the safe for now."

The next day Mervyn was there when I turned up for work.

He pointed to the table. "Look at those."

There was a sheet of paper with four titles written on it:

Hamlet
The Dunciad
Wuthering Heights
Les Illuminations

I thought for a few minutes, then I suddenly saw why Mervyn existed.

"What a clever man you are," I said. "Yes, you're quite right. All books he didn't illustrate but could have done. All things within the range of his obsession."

"Are they within the range of yours, though?"

"I think so," I said. "I'll have to go and do a bit of reading, you understand, but in principle I'd say yes."

"Ever started doing Delaquays without a Delaquay in front of you?"

"No," I said, "no, I haven't. But it's the only way I can draw. I couldn't do anything else even if I tried."

"Then take off the rest of the week," he said. "Do some reading. You can come back on Monday and start working downstairs on your chosen text. You can't use this sort of paper, of course. Nor this ink. I'll provide papers and inks. I know where to get them."

"Money, Mervyn."

"Here's fifty," he said, opening the petty cash tin. "On this stuff, we'll go halves. You produce it, I'll sell it, we split the proceeds."

"A car?"

"You can have mine as soon as we've sold some. I need a newer one, anyway."

"Or an older one," I said.

I started with *The Dunciad.* It burned so bright with detestation. The skin of the poem itched with such loathing at the cultural functionaries of Pope's time, I found myself laughing with recognition. Things hadn't changed very much. Lines like, "And pond'rous slugs cut swiftly through the sky" or the couplet:

> *Unstain'd, untouch'd, and yet in maiden sheets*
> *While all your smutty sisters walk the streets*

had me reaching for my pen. Then I remembered that I wasn't to do anything until Mervyn had provided me with the necessary materials. And I started pondering the implications of all this. I'd become nervous by the time I arrived back at the gallery the next week.

"How many years would you get for faking Delaquays, Mervyn?"

"My dear fellow, don't ever let me hear you use that word again.

"A fake, incidentally, in the usual meaning is a picture carrying a signature which is not the name of the person who made the picture. So that's the first definition dispensed with, since Delaquay didn't sign his works and you're not going to either. A fake is usually also thought of as a cunningly reproduced copy of an existing work of some value. You're not copying anything and would you mind telling me what the value of a Delaquay is, since no one has been allowed to sell them?

"One of the hardest categories to deal with in art has always been 'school of,' where disciples and apprentices learn their craft from the master and then work in his manner, often helping with the master's own work. Is that faking—learning how to place a line thus, cut a piece of metal so, color the sky with that degree of subtlety?"

"All completely innocent, then, is it, Mervyn?"

"Undoubtedly."

"So why do I have to use these special materials you've acquired?"

"So your own working methods might approximate as closely as possible to those of Delaquay. It's interesting, you know, but over the last few years late-Victorian sketchbooks have become very popular. The odd thing is that the ones with the most blank pages left in them fetch the best prices in the auction houses. Why do you think that might be, Tom?"

I worked downstairs in the cellar. It was comfortable enough though gloomy. I could see up into the street through a small opening. I could see the feet going back and forth, tap-tapping their repeated journeys. These crowds without faces helped me with *The Dunciad*. Day by day the images fell into place. Where Pope had

> *A fire, a jigg, a battle, and a ball,*
> *Till one wide conflagration swallows all*

I used the plague dance-of-death and the Great Fire. Infection and apocalypse.

Mervyn was particularly taken with my images of the Queen of Dulness. "She's real," he said. "There's some real hate there somewhere."

"She's my mother."

There were echoes of Bosch certainly in some of these pen drawings, but then he'd played his part in Delaquay's iconography. The witches from Dürer were my idea, but there was no reason why they shouldn't have been there. In fact, the more I worked the more confident I became that my decisions were the right ones. I didn't need to consult anything but my own judgment and experience. I finished all the drawings for *The Dunciad* in two weeks.

Then I started on Rimbaud's *Season in Hell*. This was Blake's journey but made by a true Catholic. This hell was no dialectical inversion.
As Rimbaud himself said, theology was no joke. The untaxed liquor
from Satan's distillery was poison, but it was the poison that made
visions possible. This had been Delaquay's world. Now it was mine. This
filthiness and exaltation I had made my own. This thing of darkness I'd
finally acknowledged.

I realized that within years of Rimbaud writing "J'ai horreur de tous
les métiers" Gerard Manley Hopkins was writing in joyous celebration
of "all trades, their gear and tackle and trim." Rimbaud could have been
a priest. In his own way perhaps he was. I drew him as the altar boy gazing at that miracle with bread and wine, then later sharing the poisoned
chalice with Verlaine as they knotted sheets between them. The lowest
taverns of Paris and London. Those Doré illustrations I had looked at so
carefully with Rachel, for my own project on hell, all came back into my
mind. I drew as though I had never done anything else for the whole of
my life.

"I need another fifty pounds, Mervyn," I said, without looking up as
I heard him come down the stairs.

"What did you do with the last lot?"

"Spent it on research."

"What are you researching?"

"Rimbaud's *Season in Hell*."

"I see," he said. He was standing behind my back. "That's good,
Tom, that's remarkable. A hint of Aubrey Beardsley perhaps, but with
your own menace."

"Fifty pounds, Mervyn, there's still time to get to the bank."

And off he went. He needed me now. I liked that.

That night I went into town. I took the Rimbaud with me in my pocket.
The clattering of shoes on the pavement above me in the gallery still carried on its sinister tattoo. It seemed to be a permanent noise inside my
head. Strangely, though, I didn't mind it. I saw the figures of hell all

around me, flashing briefly among the bottles in the mirrors behind bars. Doors opened down to cellars or up to lofts. Rimbaud had walked these streets while he wrote his infernal meditation. The only difference was that Satan had increased his taxes on the poisons.

"Do you want to come up, darling?"

About Donna's age, I suppose. She would look older if the light were bright upstairs. They always did. Blond. Black skirt, black stockings, white blouse. Unbuttoning herself already.

"You'll have to give me the money first."

Stepping out of her skirt. The white flash of thighs above the black.

"Who do you want me to be?"

"The one who comes in the night."

"Ah, then lie back there and close your eyes."

The next morning I felt bad. There was a cupboard in Mervyn's cellar where he kept the drink. I found a bottle of gin. No tonic. I drank a glass straight and it made me feel a little better. Then on I went with Rimbaud, the catechized demonologist. There was nothing he said that didn't make perfect sense to me. It all made Delaquay's sense. But then these days *I* made Delaquay's sense. There was a preoccupation with alchemy in the Rimbaud to which I addressed myself. I used some of the symbols. Mostly, though, to conjure his world of dementia and intoxication, I used memory.

"I can't do any more," I told Mervyn. "That's the Rimbaud."

"They're good," he said. "Very good indeed."

"Giles Astley," I said.

"My uncle. Wrote a book, I think. Something odd. Never read it. Taken up by Isaac Lenau."

"*The Sustaining Wound,*" I said. "First book I ever read at the Institute. What happened to him?"

"Terrible business. He was an officer in the Great War, you know. Out at the front. Lost his memory. Spent the last forty years of his life in a nursing home in Surrey. Only died a while back. Completely gaga. Couldn't even pee unless a nurse held his willy for him."

"I need a break before I start the other two," I said. "*Hamlet* and *Wuthering Heights*. Think I'd better have a little trip to Yorkshire. Those moors."

"Suit yourself," Mervyn said equably, turning over the drawings I'd done. "How are you going to get there?"

"Thought I'd drive your car."

17

In the Bleak Midwinter

Who scorched with excessive heat
  Such floods of tears did shed
As though His floods should quench His flames
  Which with His tears were fed.
ROBERT SOUTHWELL, "The Burning Babe"

IT TOOK ME A WHILE TO GET USED TO THE GEAR CHANGE, THEN I started to sense the power under the bonnet. Mervyn was going to have to buy himself another Jaguar—I was keeping this one. I hammered up the A1. It was late January and the farther north I went the chillier it started to look. When I finally got to the Cow and Calf, I climbed out of the car. I'd forgotten how cold it could be up here.

I looked at that great stone sphinx crouched on the moorside, overlooking the white valley. The sky was massed above it in gray judgment. I honestly don't know why I started crying. Perhaps it was the proximity of Grimshaw and Agatha and the realization that I couldn't possibly go and stay with them. Wasn't I betraying everything they stood for at this moment? Or maybe it was the proximity of my own childhood, which can often reduce a man to tears. I wasn't sure where I'd left my childhood but these moors were as good a place as any to start looking. The wind slapped my face and cooled my cheek.

I walked up to the hotel there and booked myself in for the night. A room with a view onto the moor, I said. Onto the Cow and Calf. Ten minutes later I was sitting by the window with a whiskey in my hand.

The whiskey warmed me, quelled me, though I couldn't have told you what it was that needed quelling.

It was an Egyptian sphinx, not the talkative Greek one with wings. I watched it as the light died. It was the Greek one who had put puzzles to Oedipus and then thrown herself from the precipice when he answered correctly. This Egyptian one said nothing, but stared out over the black and white landscape guarding the memories. It was only recently I'd discovered that the Egyptian sphinx is male.

I pulled the table over to the window and started drawing. I drew and drew. But my sphinx was female, and with an ageless smile. She stared out over the sands and the sands said nothing.

The next morning I parked the car outside Robert Southwell and walked in. I had forgotten nothing. In the chapel I knelt and tried to say a prayer, but how could I pray now? Where could I start? I would have to go to confession and that would involve setting my soul against any further sin, or the absolution would be worthless. Rimbaud knew: they have baptized me into damnation, he said. There is no escape from the order of my christening. They have set the seal on my destruction. In my bag in the Jaguar were the drawings I had made the night before. I was going to use them for the Brontë. My resolution seemed all set in a direction away from absolution. In the apse I looked again at those diagrammatic paintings of Christ's scourging. I'd never noticed before the little spiteful demons peering over the shoulders of the Roman torturers. I suppose it was a normal day's business for both of them.

I stopped at the end of the street where Grimshaw's house was. I couldn't face him. The savagery of that intelligence still daunted me. This scourging I would have to postpone, until the next life possibly. I drove over to Haworth to see the stretch of moor where Emily's imagination had exploded. The snow came frittering and tumbling from the sky. I could have spent some days here but decided to head back south. London was where I belonged, with Mervyn and Cork Street and the prospect of money.

But first I drove over to Jervaulx. It looked exactly the same. No reason for it not to. It had survived four hundred years, why should a few more alter it? I could still see Grimshaw starting on the long lecture that he gave me throughout all the years I was with him. Grimshaw. I remembered what his hand felt like in mine. All I could feel coming was the slap of his palm against my cheek.

I drove hard back down to London. At ninety the car handled well but was noisy. I parked in Soho. I needed a woman, except I was aware that it wasn't any of these women I needed. Thrusting and thrashing with them I could forget for a while whatever it was I really did need.

I had my own keys to the gallery now and I was there before Mervyn on Monday morning. Working too. Working furiously at the Brontë. It was all moors and lethal weather. The occasional echo of a distant figure underneath the wind, as though arguing with the sky itself. The gods in *Wuthering Heights* are primal forces, untainted by morality.

"Good trip?" Mervyn asked, when he came in.

"Satisfactory," I said.

"Car go all right?"

"Fine," I said. "I'm keeping it. Go buy another. I'll have the Brontë finished by the end of the week."

I noticed the cabinet now contained whiskey, gin, brandy, beer, tonic, and soda. How very nice, I thought. Mervyn has decided to cater for my needs.

By the end of the week I'd finished the Brontë. Now there was only *Hamlet* left. I made Donna into Ophelia and Henry VIII into Claudius. I was about to emerge through the door into the gallery when I heard Mervyn talking.

"I have a dwarf in the cellar painting me some Rembrandts," he said, and giggled. The squall of English public schoolboy laughter. Two tall men from the Household Cavalry. I made Rosencrantz and Guildenstern into twins and both of their faces were Mervyn's. Both were bald and fatuously grinning. In time I'd show him.

I couldn't separate Hamlet from Grimshaw, so ceaseless had that pre-occupation been with him, so often had he ranted at me, in school and out. I started from his face and tried to unflesh the years from those features. I removed the age from Grimshaw's skin and that younger man became my Hamlet. I made him a clown, in whiteface there against the black velvet of his own melancholy. Death's truth amid the graveyard jokes.

I was finished. Two hundred drawings.

"I've done, Mervyn," I shouted up at him. I was already pouring myself a drink from his cabinet.

"Remarkable," he murmured to himself as he rustled through them. "How very clever!" He stopped at the Rosencrantz and Guildenstern, those twin apes of Shakespeare's pursy times.

"That'll have to come out," he said.

"What's the matter? Not flattering enough?"

"Delaquay and I were not acquainted so it might seem a little odd if . . ."

"Suit yourself," I said. "That's my part finished."

"Not quite, I'm afraid. There's the matter of the catalog. We want an extensive one for this show. You'll have to write it."

I stared at him.

"Well, who else is going to do it?"

"How long?"

"A thousand words. Two if you could manage it. Do you have anything on the subject?"

"Only in my head," I said, "though I suppose there's a fair bit there. I doubt the Delaquay Society would give me access to its Proceedings for the purposes specified."

"It seems a little unlikely."

"When do you need it?"

"Monday. I've scheduled the exhibition for next month. Do cheer up, Tom. Think of the money."

"Give me the Milton and the Dante and the Baudelaire, so I have something to trigger my memory." Then I picked up his car keys, which were lying on the table, and went off in the Jaguar. The next Monday morning at nine o'clock I placed the pieces of paper on his desk and left again before he arrived. The walls were covered with Delaquay illustrations of books he never illustrated. I looked at them closely. They had aged since they left my hand. Little brown foxings. Mervyn. I placed the three books he did illustrate back on the shelf.

Catalog

Delaquay Society Illustrations

Alfred Delaquay is one of the most mysterious figures the world of art has ever known. A man of large private means, he never had to concern himself with considerations that affect most other artists at least at the beginning of their careers: seeking commissions or patrons, exhibiting their work. During the very period when the mass reproduction of works of art became a matter of course, his books were printed in editions of no more than three, sometimes only of one.

Delaquay was a recluse so far as the world of art and publicity was concerned, though his hermitage was the streets of Paris and London. Delaquay's work, so far as we know, consisted entirely of illustrations for books, very particular books which had great significance for him. They were often books riddled with the dark themes of man's fall and the demonic power of the rebellious angels.

An early experience of the power of handmade books in the shape of a French book of hours led Delaquay to believe that a unique force accrued to such a creation, a specific potency dispelled as soon as the book should be printed by machine in large numbers. Hence his strategy. Working with specialized printers on exquisite papers, he tipped in his original line drawings or engravings.

Perhaps most extraordinary of all, once these books had been created, they could not then be bought. Delaquay expressly forbade any dealings involving money in regard to his work. The books circulated only through the Delaquay Society itself, whose members were not allowed to have any of them reproduced, on penalty of expulsion.

It is not known how many books Delaquay illustrated. More work has recently been coming to light.

By the time this appeared in the front of the catalog Mervyn had added something to it:

It has been known for a long time that the only other works by Delaquay outside the books were his own working copies, more often than not as remarkable as the finished works themselves. It is a collection of these which was recently discovered in a Parisian attic. The Astley Gallery is proud to be able to offer these to the public. This is the first time that Delaquay's work has been on sale anywhere in the world.

The signature at the bottom read: "Thomas Lynch, onetime Archivist of the Delaquay Society."

18

The New Age

It was the best of times, it was the worst of times.
CHARLES DICKENS, *A Tale of Two Cities*

I LIKED TO WALK TO WORK WHEN THE WEATHER WAS FINE. LONDON had come alive since I'd first arrived there. Now, as I made my way up one street and down another, I saw the clothes exploding and heard the music as it started leaking out of shops and boutiques. The Beatles, the Stones, Dylan. It was a good time to be around, as long as you had plenty of hair. That was a key requirement. It simply wasn't a decade to go bald in. Poor old Mervyn! I'd seen him give his mirror a wounded look. His double-breasted suit had an old-fashioned air about it too. He gave the impression of being nothing so much as a mildly disreputable son of the *ancien régime,* which in truth was precisely what he was.

He prepared for the coming exhibition though. He did know how to use the telephone and the dinner table, and he used both assiduously for the next four weeks. On the day of the opening, he turned up in a new red Jaguar, exactly the same model, a 3.4, but fresh from the showroom.

"You might at least have chosen another rubric, Mervyn," I said.

"I'm a man of constant tastes," he said. "I have borrowed the money for this motor car, so considerable is my faith in the success of what we are launching."

He had put a price of two hundred pounds on all 199 drawings.

"Optimistic," I said.

"You just watch."

I did.

The opening night was divided between those who had heard that the new age had started and those who hadn't. The latter, still dressed in tight-fitting suits and silk ties with grease around the knot, were already walking about in their own shadow, but the shadow was illuminated now by the polka-dot shirts, bright jeans, Cuban heels, miniskirts, and bright bandannas of the children of Aquarius. The only thing that hadn't changed much between them was the quality of the comments. I drifted about with my glass in my hand.

"There's an obvious debt to Ingres. Look at the drawing of that face."

(There was no debt to Ingres unless you count the fact that he and Delaquay both liked drawing with a pen.)

"There's an art nouveau curvature to the lines."

(There wasn't. Very deliberately wasn't.)

"I think I can see the extent to which he was reacting against photography."

(No such reaction ever took place.)

Inevitably the most fatuous comments were delivered in the loudest voices, to give most benefit to the ignorant in the room. I had heard so often in that place the languid drawl in which they delivered their *aperçus*. Keep smiling and nodding, Mervyn had said, make sure they sign the check. Tonight I neither smiled nor nodded. Mervyn did, though, more than I've ever seen before. The little blue disks were turning into pink ones. Money was being handed over. Addresses were being written down.

The gallery was full so I didn't actually notice when Bill and Donna arrived. They had young Tom with them. Nearly seven now. He wasn't quite the dismal grizzler I remembered from the day of his baptism, but he still had a disgruntled look about him. And he still wasn't as pretty as his mother. Or his father either, if it came to that.

Donna renewed her sibling ties with Mervyn while Bill walked about. I could see the look on his face. He was impressed, although I sensed that he didn't want to be. Finally he saw me.

"Hello, Bill."

"Tom, how smart you look." (I was wearing my gallery suit.) "Some exhibition you have here."

"Like it, do you, Bill?"

"Like is hardly the word."

We looked at each other. Beaumont Street. Jericho. Donna.

"I'm intrigued to know more about the attic in Paris where all this was found. I thought I knew the Paris members, thought I knew them all—even the dead ones. Obviously the Astley Gallery could show the Delaquay Society a thing or two in this respect."

Eyes still friendly, but not as friendly as they once were. Something had darkened in my old friend Bill, and I had a feeling I knew what it was.

"You'd have to ask Mervyn all that," I said. "All a mystery to me too, I'm afraid. He simply showed me the first five or six and I said they were obviously Delaquays."

"Didn't consider contacting us? To give the Society a chance to acquire them and so hold on to its identity?"

"Well, Bill, there's all sorts of identities to hang on to. Mervyn seems to think that his depends on a new Jaguar from time to time. I'm not sure I have one at all anymore. Last time I had anything like an identity I was living in Oxford. In Beaumont Street. Before my departure, that is."

We could both hear Donna's laughter. I took his empty glass and went over with it to the drinks table. On the way Mervyn grabbed my arm.

"Marvelous. This is marvelous. We're going to sell fifty by the end of the evening. Fifty! On the first day."

I had never seen Mervyn so beatific. Money really did have the most soothing effect upon his soul.

"I've asked Donna and Bill to come and join us at Luigi's for a meal after. They've not eaten."

"That will include the child, will it?"

"Unless you want to put him in the cellar."

One too many Toms, I thought.

In the restaurant Mervyn ordered Chianti with the meal. Bill and I stared at the bottle and then at each other.

"To memories of Firenze, then, Bill."

He raised his glass.

"And the memory of Alfred Delaquay, who has made all this, and so much more, possible."

"Yes, indeed," Mervyn said loudly. "And may we toast the eminence of the two Archivists of the Delaquay Society we are honored to have at our table. It's hard enough to talk to one usually. To have two at the same time seems almost *de trop.*"

"It does, doesn't it?" Bill said, still looking at me. Unsmiling.

"Almost," I said, and chinked his glass with mine. "I suppose you can have too much of a good thing."

By this time Donna was chirruping loudly at Mervyn.

"So it's going to be a success, then?"

"Indubitably. A great success. My prediction is that we will sell out. Press coverage. Wouldn't even surprise me if there weren't a program on the radio. I suppose I should apologize, Bill, we've rent the veil of your temple."

"Oh, I shouldn't worry too much," Bill said. "I suppose it had to be rent by someone sooner or later. You've reproduced them," he said, looking at me now. "You've put them in a catalog. There's a flaming brand at the gate of Eden."

"Maybe it was time to let a bit of air in, Bill."

"Maybe it was time to let a bit of money in, Tom. My students want to talk more and more about money. Interesting that. They come for philosophy sessions and then they end up talking to me about Marx and class society. I said to them to begin with, Marx is incompatible with philosophy. He said it himself. The philosophers only interpret when the point is to change. But maybe Marx was right, though I suspect the class society will turn out to be longer lasting than him:

> *"The young Marx was once heard to say*
> *Let the proles bawl and bicker away.*
> *Think I give a toss*
> *Which class is the boss?*
> *I'll be published in Penguin one day.*

"What do you think now, Tom? Do you think everything finally comes down to money too?"

"No," I said, "unless you don't have any. Then unfortunately it does. How salt is the taste of another man's bread and how hard it is to walk up and down his stairs."

"Dante. Mervyn's Dante."

"I had thought it was Delaquay's," I said.

"Maybe we should now talk about Mervyn's Delaquays."

Donna's voice was beginning to soar with elation. "You'll have to expand," she said. "You'll probably need another assistant."

"Certainly. Tom can't be regarded as an assistant anymore."

"I could fill in for a while," Donna said. "We could use the money."

"And young Tom . . ."

"He could stay with his aunt in Oxford during the week."

Young Tom was starting to doze. Luigi came and took him out to the back with a blanket wrapped around him.

"Look over there," said Mervyn, pointing out of the window. "See those two red Jaguars. One is Tom's and one's mine."

To be made kindred to Mervyn, even via a motor car, doused my thoughts with a chilly wave for a moment. I would find out the price of a respray.

"May we all live in interesting times," said Bill, raising his glass.

■

As they left in their taxi toward the station, Bill put his head through the window.

"I believe Grimshaw is making his way down here to see the exhibition. Told him he'd probably have an opportunity to talk to you finally."

I turned to Mervyn as the cab drove off. "You're not going to take Donna on in the gallery, are you?"

"Don't see why not. She was the one, after all, who talked me into setting *you* on. And look how well that's turned out."

We walked along for a moment in silence.

"What you should be thinking about, Tom," he said, "are the contents of the next Paris attic we discover."

I stopped walking and looked at him. "I'm not doing any more," I said.

"Come, come," he said. "Often the virgin after her deflowering has been heard to cry that she'll never ever do *that* again. But as another Thomas used to say, After the first death there is no other."

19

Dissolution

HAMLET: *What looked he? Frowningly?*
HORATIO: *A countenance more in sorrow than in anger.*
WILLIAM SHAKESPEARE, *Hamlet.* Act I, Scene 2

MERVYN WAS IN FESTIVE MOOD. A BOTTLE OF CHAMPAGNE WAS often on his desk, with glasses ready to be filled arranged in a little circle about it. I would sit in the cellar, watching the television set that Mervyn had installed down there. Vietnam. The Beatles. Men strung out in space, an umbilical cord tying them to the mother ship. The murder of Diem. The first self-immolations by Buddhist monks. Sitting so perfectly still in the lotus position as the flames melted their faces. Between the pull-down bed, the radio, the television, and the drinks cabinet, it was starting to feel comfortable underground.

I didn't know Grimshaw was in the gallery. It was only when Mervyn appeared and motioned me up with his quiet "Old fellow wants to see you" that I remembered Bill's prediction.

He had a walking stick. The left side of him was sluggish as he dragged himself around. He was peering at each image intently. I let him complete his tour. When he turned and saw me I realized that his face was even thinner, if that were possible. The flesh appeared translucent, showing a map of veins beneath. But the eyes bored into me with exactly the same intensity. He held out his hand. I went over and took it in mine. When he spoke there was a slight blur to his words.

"Well, Tom, you're looking very dapper. Life in the West End of London evidently agrees with you."

I looked down at the stick and the quivering hand that gripped it so tightly.

"Stroke, I'm afraid. Not quite as mobile as I was. Are these by Delaquay?"

The suddenness of the question startled me.

"I . . . I don't know."

"Think I do. Let your yes be yes and your no be no. Remember. All else comes from the evil one."

Mervyn appeared from below. He poured out two glasses of champagne and brought them over to us. Grimshaw took hold of his without enthusiasm.

"Could we interest you in a purchase? We still have nearly half the stock left but it's diminishing rapidly. You could have your own Delaquay. I would predict a one hundred percent increase in value by this time next year."

"Oh, you would, would you?" Grimshaw said, staring at Mervyn with evident distaste. "Well, it's very good of you to keep some for me but I'll decline your offer all the same. My house has many Delaquays in it—not mine, you understand. Not anyone's if it comes to that. That is the whole point, or was a little while back.

"In any case I must be making my way to the station. I only came here to satisfy a certain curiosity. Now I'll go and catch my train. Thank you so much for this champagne. Would you mind very much if I don't drink it? No criticism of its provenance, you understand. Perhaps young Tom here might finish my glass. I daresay he's rather more used to the stuff than I."

He started to limp toward the door with considerable effort. I held it open for him and stepped out onto the pavement behind him.

"Let me get my car keys," I said. "I'll drive you to the station."

"One of those red jobs is yours, is it?"

"The older one."

I went back in but by the time I came out again he was already climbing into a taxi. I helped heave him in and onto the seat.

"Won't you let me drive you?"

"There's really no need," he said, settling back into the seat. "Agatha would like to see you of course, as would I come to that, should you ever venture north again. But don't come in that thing," he said, pointing to the car. "Altogether the wrong color to park next to millstone grit."

I reached in and took his hand.

"She still makes very good dumplings, you know. To King's Cross, please, driver."

The cab pulled away. I went back into the gallery.

"Delaquay Society, I suppose?" Mervyn said blithely. "Have his champagne, anyway, before it starts to go flat. No point worrying about these people, you know."

"He's not these people."

"What?"

"Give me a hundred pounds, Mervyn, and shut up."

"I don't have a hundred."

"Go and get it, then. Or would you prefer me to take back all my Delaquays, even the ones with the little pink circles on?"

He went to the bank.

And that night I went to Soho. I took three purple hearts from my little bottle in Paddington, to quicken myself up a little, then I set out on my trawl around the bars.

Delaquay Proceedings, Volume Seven

During the years of his addiction, Delaquay's naturally obsessive mind darkened into a state we might now describe as psychopathological. The sexual hunt and the sexual act became iconic, became images of perverse meditation and inverted worship. He was only too aware of the spiritual dangers of all this. Indeed, it was the dangers themselves that he courted so assiduously. He used all this experience in his most questionable works. The circle he moved in would have regarded a term like "pornography" with contempt. For them that was a reference to the law, while they were lords of the imagination.

We might now perhaps see a certain irony in their scorn of the bourgeoisie, these children of bourgeois homes living off their bourgeois inheritances. Some worked hard, though, not despite their self-imposed degradation, but as it were through it. Baudelaire was one of these. So too was Delaquay. Like the chiffonnier *himself, they picked up the refuse of society and formed it into a new whole, employing their own bodies as a basis on which to mount the spectacle.*

■

Ferguson was in the French.

"Whiskey?" he said. I nodded.

"Lots of whiskey, eh, Tom, then out after the creatures of the night. Some of the older ones think you're a very good thing indeed, I gather. Most men only spend money on women younger than the ones they can get at home. But not so with you, they tell me."

Ferguson wasn't interested in women at all. And so he had developed a dispassionate, anthropological sort of interest in those who were. He was only an inch taller than I was. Black hair, the whole of one eye twisted upward where the broken end of a bottle had screwed into it. He was a painter committed to total abstraction, a follower of the lowland puritanism of Mondrian. So they said anyway.

"You should get your partner in crime to introduce you to the Billet. That's where Mervyn goes when he can't keep his flies buttoned. Plenty of older women there would provide services for nothing, I'd have thought. One or two might do it for even less. Or perhaps you can't get a stiffy unless a cash transaction's involved? I've known fellows like that. . . . Tumescence never was *my* problem, you understand. My problem's always been trying to keep the bugger down—as the Metropolitan Police could inform you. Strange how fetching the boys in blue look in black stockings."

Outside again. Circling the streets, looking for something entirely new to solve your riddles. If only for half an hour. Soho. Flashing its Christmas-tree lights on and off. Another upstairs room. The pills and booze together distilling into a bite of concentration. I've noticed it before.

"Money first," she says. "Who am I supposed to be tonight?"

"A woman in an upstairs room who takes her clothes off and says nothing."

I woke up in the cellar of the gallery. I'd left my flat keys down there and by the time I arrived I couldn't face the rest of the journey. I was awake when Mervyn came in, though "awake" is too mild a word to describe the parched scream in my head. There was another pill I often took to put me out again but all my pills were in Paddington.

Drinks cupboard. I scanned the bottles there to work out what I might be able to swallow without vomiting. Vodka and orange juice. My hand shook as I sipped it. Upstairs Mervyn's patter was already slicking away. Another devotee of Delaquay was being propositioned. With the help of three vodkas I managed to get back to sleep around ten.

In the afternoon I went up into the gallery. I hadn't shaved.

"You look terrible," Mervyn said. "Where were you last night?"

"Soho."

"Researching, I suppose. Go home."

"I'm going."

I was making for the door when Rachel arrived. Streaks of gray in her hair now, like foam in the cascade. Dark clothes still bobbined tightly round her. She was even more beautiful than the last time I'd seen her. The years between had simplified her. The pure fact of her face and body.

"I came to look for myself," she said. "There are so many rumors in Oxford."

"Down at the bottom of the road there on the left," I said. "There's a little pub. I'll wait for you in it."

After half an hour she came.

"I'm sorry," I said.

"Apologizing to me or the Delaquay Society?"

"Maybe to both."

"You haven't shaved."

"Artist's privilege. Delaquay grew a beard."

"I must go in a minute, Tom, I have a train to catch. Lectures to-morrow."

"Let me drive you to Oxford," I said. "I have a car now."

Most of the way we drove in silence. It was a pleasant evening, cruising up through the wooded avenues of the A40. When we arrived I left the engine running and walked around to the passenger side.

"You could have a coffee," she said.

"When's the end of term?"

"Next week."

"You remember that picture of Bolton Abbey by Turner? First thing you ever showed us."

She nodded.

"Would you like to see it? The place itself? We could drive up. You'd like it there, it's beautiful."

"Tom, you must try to understand something—"

"I'll be here at nine in the morning next Saturday. With the engine running. I'll wait ten minutes then drive off. I'm going up there anyway. I need to. I have to find my way back to something. If you want to come, I'd very much like you to come."

That week I sobered up. Took no pills. Went for walks in the park. I tried to concentrate on my life, but that was too hard so I concentrated on Rachel instead. The next Saturday at nine o'clock I parked the car outside her flat and kept the engine running. Two minutes later she came out carrying her large leather bag. That looked older too.

And so it was that Mr. and Mrs. Lynch checked that night into the big hotel above the Cow and Calf. When I went into the bathroom in the morning, the soap had already gone. I rubbed her salts and herbs into my skin and remembered that smell.

I drove her back and forth across Yorkshire as Grimshaw had once driven me. We would catch glimpses through the car window. Sheep's fleece on barbed wire. Rusting wheels and axles in a disused works yard. So many of the mills already dead, mourning in black millstone grit, blind and boarded windows looming from a hundred feet in the air. A gypsy's white horse walked the circle of its tether in a slanted field. Washing waving bleakly from the clotheslines. Finally we parked the car two hundred yards from Bolton Abbey.

"We're here," I said.

"So show me around."

When I finally walked back into that ruined Gothic nave, I was holding Rachel's hand.

"Ruins," Rachel said, looking at the tracery on a section of standing wall. "According to Lenau, that's all that history ever gives us. There is no history of art, there is only a catalog of ruins. A ruin represents a particularly acute form of truth: it is what time shakes us down to."

"Time was given a fair bit of assistance in the task here," I said.

"Not many died," she said. "Millions didn't die. I can never understand what all the fuss is about."

"Truth, I suppose."

"Truth is a ruin too," she said. "At least you're allowed to walk around inside it, even if you can't hear the plainchant anymore. There've been worse catastrophes than the ones that affected you people. There are plenty of flatter ruins than this.

"Interesting the way Turner rearranged it, isn't it? Maybe painting is the ruin of topography."

"Maybe the imagination is the ruin of science," I said.

"That's Blake," she said. "But science is another exercise of the imagination. It simply has to spend more time reconsidering itself and doing the measurements."

It was lunchtime. I thought for a moment.

"Rachel, I think you're going to find the vegetarian diet up here a little limited. It'll largely be meat and two veg without the meat."

We went to find out in the nearest pub. In fact she had cheese salad. And Tetley's bitter, for which she was developing a taste.

I was standing at the window. You could see the outline of the sphinx's shoulder against the moonlit sky. She was in bed, murmuring mostly to herself, turned away from me.

"It's not what's hidden in there that's the problem," she said. "It's the hiding is the problem, Tom. We all have a bag of rats to carry round our necks all our lives. The problem is pretending it's not there."

"She was silent mostly," I said after a while. "When she spoke it was often to herself. Vindictive whispers. She said over and over, 'If I had to be given a child, why couldn't it have been a girl at least? Your father left you inside me,' she said, 'then fell out of the sky on fire. Should never have been up there anyway. Don't touch me,' she said, 'I was touched before by someone called Tom Lynch and my life's been ruined ever since. Don't get in the bed,' she said, 'go back to your own bed, the nightmare's finished. For you at least. And do stop that wretched crying, child.'

"I had this bird. A white bird. No brothers or sisters, just a bird. How she hated that bird. One day I came down and it was dead in its cage. She said it had hanged itself on the chain of its mirror. Just carried on eating her toast. 'Don't say you're going to cry over that now,' she said, 'it was only a bird.' Then a dog. Ate poison and died. I cried. Couldn't stop crying. 'A big boy like you crying,' she said, 'even a girl would be tougher than that. Look what your father left me with, a boy who'll never be a man, who can't stop crying.'"

"How do you think the animals died, Tom?" Her voice half asleep from the bed.

"I don't know."

"She probably killed them, don't you think? At least one of them anyway. You know. You've always known. All you have to do is acknowledge that you know, then you can stop running away from the knowledge. You only need to hate your maggot-bag of a mother for a while, then you'll be able to stop hating her. And yourself.

"It was the same with Lenau. His madness came from that, I think. He could almost admit it, but not quite. He said, all children live in a state of primal terror only assuaged by the arrival of the mother in the dark. Yours didn't turn up and I don't think his did either. It could have been worse. She didn't kill you. She wasn't Medea. Your mother didn't love you at all and you're both alive. My parents loved me with all their hearts and they're both dead."

"Will you marry me, Rachel?"

"I'm twelve years older than you and I don't have a womb. I'm a Jew, you're a Roman Catholic. You could probably find an easier way to get yourself married. I can't be your mother, Tom."

"I don't want you to be my mother. I've had one, and one was enough. I want you to be my wife."

"A wife without a womb."

"There are worse things a woman can be missing."

"You'll have to give up faking Delaquays."

"I already have."

"No meat in the house."

"Or soap."

"Not a Catholic wedding."

"It seems unlikely, what with your previous engagement."

"You'll grow to hate me as you see me getting older so much quicker than you. Old men chase young girls so they can forget the grave. You'll see the grave looking at you every time you sit down for breakfast."

"And not even any meat on the plate."

"Or any soap in the sink. And where do we live?"

"In Oxford. I want to finish that thesis I started on the topography of hell. Remember?"

"Oh, I remember. Planning on earning any money? I don't have much."

"I have ten thousand pounds due to me shortly from Mr. Mervyn Astley. That should get us somewhere to live. Time enough to finish my thesis. Could I get a job at the Lenau, do you think?"

"Maybe. If you stay sober. There was a rumor once that you were our most promising student."

"I might get drunk sometimes."

"And when you do it will always be your elderly wife who drove you to it. Come to bed and leave that stone-hearted sphinx up there to take care of the moors. You've thought about her enough for one lifetime. I don't mind someone called Tom Lynch getting into *my* bed, even if you did lie about my name to the man in reception."

"You don't mind me being so short?" I said, as she wrapped her legs around me.

"No. All my life I've tried to keep my head down. You don't even need to bend your neck."

The next morning we went down to see the swastika stone.

"It's alive," Rachel said. "I'd no idea it was so fluent and organic. All curves and purpose. Lenau insisted that life was a progression from terror to its amelioration in controlling images. But here it's the other way around. All the civilization lay in the Bronze Age. They made the stone come alive. The Nazis killed it into geometry and death."

It had rained during the night. The lower incisions had collected water. She dipped her finger in one, then put it into her mouth. Then she dipped her finger in again.

"Come over here," she said. Then she put her finger into my mouth.

"We're going to call on Patrick and Agatha Grimshaw down in the village."

"Why's that?"

"I want to introduce them to my future wife."

I left the car a few streets away. I could imagine Grimshaw's face at the window if I parked in front of his house with that red Jaguar.

He stood there in the doorway, gripping his stick.

"Why, Tom," he said. "What a surprise. Agatha, Tom's here and . . ."

"Rachel," I said. "My fiancée."

The silence gradually started to fill up with noise as little awkward questions were asked and then answered.

"Will it be . . . will it be a church wedding?"

"I'm afraid not," I said. "Rachel has been married before. In any case she . . . she is not a Catholic."

"I am Jewish," she said.

"Ah," said Grimshaw, "and are you of the Jewish people or the Jewish faith?"

"I believe in remembrance," she said. "I have kept that much of my faith."

"But not providence?" said Grimshaw.

"I don't know how you'd fit all the deaths into providence."

"No," Grimshaw said sadly, "no, that I can understand. I can't fit them in either, however hard I try."

"I thought your Church required it."

"My Church requires many things I'm unable to give it," Grimshaw said. "I once required something of my Church it proved unable to give too. So perhaps we balance each other out. Perhaps remembrance is all that I have saved from my faith. I'd not thought of it that way.

"In which faith would you raise the children?"

"There can be no children. An operation . . ."

"Ah! You will stay for lunch? Do you like dumplings?"

"*Knodel*? Yes."

We ate the meal and Agatha looked intensely at Rachel. I remembered how she'd once looked at me that way, sitting at the same table. Afterward they spoke together as Grimshaw and I stood out in the back garden.

"Do you think there will be any further expansion in the known works of Delaquay?"

"No," I said. "No, I don't."

"Is that a solemn undertaking?"

"It's one that my marriage is based on."

"Good. Then I think the matter should be dropped. The Society had wondered if it should . . . well, no need even to discuss it now. It's a shame about there being no possibility of children."

"Yes," I said. "Though there are worse things that can happen, perhaps."

"Perhaps."

"I'm taking Rachel up to see the cup and ring marks. Then we must head south again. Rachel has a lecture to give tomorrow morning."

"At the Lenau?"

"Yes, I'm thinking of rejoining. Finishing my studies there."

"That would be good," Grimshaw said, and smiled. The first time I could remember seeing that smile in so many years.

"You will come back and see us now?"

"Now, yes. Before it wasn't possible."

"I understand."

As we left Agatha gave me a kiss on the cheek. Then she turned and, with great solemnity, gave Rachel one too.

We stumbled about on top of the rocks looking at the cup and ring markings.

"No one really knows what they were?"

"No," I said. "All sorts of theories, but nobody knows."

On the way back in the car Rachel made me tell her how I had come into the hands of Grimshaw and Agatha. She fell silent for some time.

"You do realize," she said finally, "how much like him you look?"

20

Rachel's Lecture

Jacob is the flesh that wrestles the angelic spirit of the Absolute.
The sand is printed with the sacred runes of their struggle. But by
dawn the traces have been kicked almost back to incoherence.
The ruin of the writing we can still make out we call tradition.
ISAAC LENAU, *Marginalia,* 128

"WHAT ARE YOU LECTURING ON?" I ASKED HER AS WE WALKED
up the street toward the Lenau.

"Ruins."

It was strange to be back in that room again, and to watch Rachel
step up to the lectern. I remembered my first day there, remembered the
eerie excitement as my world was displaced. She had started.

"Isaac Lenau once stated that ruins are the only forms we can
understand. We should perhaps explore this famous fragment from the
Marginalia a little more closely.

"Time is the element that brings us to truth, but it must ruin us in
the process, so we can find our true nature. It is this ruin of ourselves, as
time embraces and then invades us, that we come to understand as our
own relation to the truth.

"We are not at home here. All forms of natural law are based upon a
lie in this respect. For Lenau, behind all forms which the mind shapes
lies the primal terror, the blankness, the cold and dark of the universe in
which we wake to find ourselves abandoned. We counter this homeless-
ness with the tragic faculty of mimesis. The Bronze Age man who stands
on the highest rock on the moor and cuts a cup and circle into the

surface is, we can speculate, trying to relate his world to the movement of the stars. The primitive man in the cave, painting the animals he hunts, is, in this recapitulation of the animal's form, trying to find the source of the power that connects them.

"Those who would take heaven by force lay claim to God as the spirit that lies behind their mimesis. They are named by the source of the violence which animates the Law. The condition of melancholy which was Lenau's intellectual fate consists of the admission that the contradictoriness in existence cannot be resolved, and that our own wish to be a name spoken by the sacred mouth must be postponed until at least our death. Perhaps thereafter too.

"Where the symbols proliferate but the agent of significance grows elusive, you have allegory, you have the Baroque, a world heavy with emblems growing ever more distant from the source of their shaping. This is the point at which melancholy can only be understood in terms of mourning.

"Mourning is the ritual by which the mind tries to bring the dead to life, but gives birth instead to remembrance. Realizing the impossibility of resurrecting that which is annihilated, it acknowledges a part of itself to be dead instead. The emblematic imagination acknowledges more and more of the world as dead. The world is a vast ruin which the intellect is condemned to interpret.

"If Shylock is portrayed by Shakespeare as a Jew ruined by his adherence to the Law, Hamlet shows us the ruin of kingship in pursuit of the truth. Truth in this world, though, is no longer compatible with absolute power, only with melancholy. The absolute ruler behaves like God set free from his own commandments, a God whose action in history can now be only violence. A God of armies. A God of concentration camps.

"As in all apparent meditations on arcana in Lenau, we find toward the end of his thought a relevance to our contemporary dilemmas. Lenau said that Fascism urges meaning onto history by placing it in uniform and telling it to shout. While Communism insists upon redemption by the relentless subjugation of experience to necessity.

"The Jewish intellectual ethos which Lenau inherited had been formed by a passage of lengthy attendance. So many centuries of waiting for a Messiah produced an incalculable subtlety in the rituals of spiritual expectation. The philology which is so crucial an element of Lenau's thought is really memory in painful precision—memory searching for a pattern amongst the shards of Kristallnacht.

"Churches exist, said Lenau, because men cannot understand the words of revelation. We might add that the cup and ring marks on the high outcrops exist because men cannot see light in the sky without being reminded of the dark all around them."

21

Payday

If tha should ever do owt for nowt,
Then do it for thisen.
YORKSHIRE SAYING

BY THE TIME I ARRIVED BACK IN LONDON I KNEW EXACTLY WHAT I was going to do. I was going to ask Mervyn for my half of the money, tell him our partnership was at an end, give notice on my flat in Paddington, and start thinking again. The lecture that morning had brought home to me how much I had abandoned my own mind since the day I'd arrived in the Astley Gallery.

Donna was at the desk when I walked in.

"Where's Mervyn?" I asked.

"At home in his flat. We tried to contact you."

"Why?"

"You'd better go and see him," she said. "You'd better talk to him yourself. It's too serious for me to explain."

Mervyn's flat was off Russell Square. He seemed to take a while to answer the door. Then he walked slowly back to the sofa and lay down.

It looked as though they had used a metal bar, something heavy and blunt anyway. Right across the top of his forehead. By now it was crosshatched with stitches.

"What happened, Mervyn?"

"It's a long story. Pour yourself a whiskey. Maybe a little brandy for me, if you wouldn't mind."

I gave him his drink but didn't take any myself. No more spirits. I had promised Rachel.

"I had some financial trouble, Tom, but you know that. You could see that I wasn't bringing any money in back there. The rent had to be paid, you know. Salaries, even small ones, had to come from somewhere.

"The bank would have simply closed me down. I knew some people. Well, to be accurate, I knew some people who knew some people. They lent me money. At pretty extensive rates of interest. That's the way they work. Well, I hadn't paid the last few installments, told them that I was really struggling. Then they got to hear about the exhibition starting to sell out, articles in the press. So they came to see me. Got a little cross, as you can see. I had to pay everything back. Or everything I could, including the interest. It comes to quite a tidy figure. I'm sorry, Tom."

"What about my ten thousand?"

"Well, it was never going to be ten thousand, now was it? There are costs in life, you know. Tax, rates, rent. Cars, gentlemen who make pictures look a little older than they were the day before. Not to mention all those advances you've been taking. There would have been a few thousand, that's for sure."

"Would have been?"

"They took it all, Tom. Look what they did. If I'd not given it to them I honestly think they'd have killed me."

"So I get nothing?"

"You have the car."

If Mervyn had not been so raw about the head I would have reached about for something to hit him with myself.

"But we'll get more out of the next one."

"What next one?"

"The next Delaquay exhibition."

"Oh no. No, no, no. That's all finished."

"I promised them, Tom."

"Then unpromise them."

"There's still money owing, you see. It's not cleared yet. The account's still outstanding because of all the interest payments. I had to tell them about you, had to, Tom. It's the only way they'd believe me that there was something still to come."

"Well, you tell them you made a mistake. No more fakes."

"You don't understand. They know who you are. I had to tell them about you. They know where you live. These are not people you can argue with. They're . . . they're very serious about money."

"I'm going, Mervyn. You won't see me anymore. Ever. So don't try to make contact. I should have known I'd never get anything out of it. Rachel is right about you."

That evening I walked about Paddington. I didn't know how to explain it to Rachel. I was still trying hard to explain it to myself. When I arrived back at the flat, the door was unlocked. I was sure I had locked it. Inside they sat in the dark, two of them, neither of them tall, but they filled up their suits.

"Sit down," the one nearest the fire said.

Then the other one leaned forward. Something bad had happened to his face once and it was all at an angle now, a little like Ferguson's, except there was no malice in Ferguson's face. There was plenty of malice in this one, and the smile only made the malice worse.

"Mr. Astley tells us that you don't intend to cooperate with the scheme he outlined to us regarding the paying off of his debts."

"That would be a real shame," the other one said, without looking at me.

"That *would* be a shame," the first continued, "because the man we represent has a very old-fashioned attitude to people who don't pay their debts."

"He takes a dim view of it, that's for sure," the other said.

"So we'd like you to perhaps reconsider what might have been a rash decision. There are many aspects to our work, some of which we find more pleasant than others."

"But we do it all. We take the rough with the smooth. We are very *conscientious.*" The other one was looking at me now. His head was shaved. There was nothing at all in his face, it was a mask.

"Some of the things that have happened with nonpayment of debts have been terrible. Do you remember that Mr. Rawnsley, Harry?"

"Oh, terrible. He was never the same again. The operations and things just couldn't get him right. The worst thing of all, though, was his wife."

"That's right, his wife. She didn't even know anything about it, but with Mr. Rawnsley not cooperating properly, well, she found herself in the line of fire."

"She was quite pretty too."

"Well, before she was."

"Before, yes, obviously. Before they took that hammer to the little twat's teeth."

"Wasn't just that, though, was it?"

"No. By the time they'd finished with her down there, she was never the same in that department either."

"Even with all the stitching up."

"No. Made a terrible mess they did, apparently. Don't think he'd have been tempted back in there."

"Like chucking a sausage up a dark alley, I should think, after they'd finished with her."

They both stood up at the same time. As they got to the door the one with the crooked face turned to me.

"Give our regards to Rachel Fein, won't you? My colleague has her address, should we ever need to . . . talk to her. Oh, nearly forgot," he said as he handed me the parcel. "Something for you. From Mervyn Astley."

I took the books from him. Then they were gone.

Rachel was shouting at me over the phone.

"Do you think this is the first time men have come for me? Haven't you noticed my accent yet? There were a lot more than two men last time. I'm telling you to leave. Now. Forget the money. Pack your bags and go. Forget Astley. Whatever happens to him, it's his problem. Come here. Now. Tonight."

She put down the phone. I looked at the books from Mervyn. One was *The Ballad of Reading Gaol.* The other was *Doctor Faustus* by Christopher Marlowe.

It wasn't loyalty to Mervyn. He could have died for all I cared about it. But I couldn't get their faces out of my mind and every time I saw them there I saw Rachel opening a door as they pushed her inside. Then I heard her screaming.

I turned up the next day at the gallery. I had the books under my arm. Donna stared at me. She was frightened too.

"I'll need some of the special paper and inks which Mervyn . . ."

"It's all downstairs," she said quietly. "It was all delivered early this morning. The drinks cupboard is full. If you need anything, you're to let me know. I'll see to it. Anything at all."

I worked. Harder than the first time. I wanted this finished.

For the Wilde I started from the Doré engraving of prisoners in their yard. A circle of Dante's hell. I remembered what Rachel had once said to me: Whenever you people set out to make heaven, you end up building hell. Reading Gaol was hell. The Astley Gallery felt like hell as well right now.

I was able to move over the paper with great speed and precision. By Friday I had completed fifty drawings for the *Ballad.* I would start again on Monday with *Doctor Faustus.* I couldn't go to Oxford, I knew that. What could I say now? I put the drawings into the safe along with the others and went up into the gallery.

"I need some money," I said.

"Yes, Mervyn said you would. There's fifty pounds in the drawer for you."

I left and headed for Soho. Ferguson was already drunk.

"The only person I ever truly loved became a Catholic priest in Dundee. It was a tragedy, really. And such a waste. He had the most wonderful thighs."

I stayed there and grew more and more drunk myself. At the end as I left Ferguson waved and leered.

"Going off to find the woman of your dreams?"

"No," I said. "No, I'm not."

I went back to the gallery. I think I was afraid to go home to Paddington. I didn't like to be in that flat anymore. I stumbled down the steps into the cellar. Didn't even put the light on. It was only when I was under the sheets that I felt her body. She'd been sleeping and I'd woken her.

"Hello," said Donna drowsily. "I wasn't sure whether or not you'd come back."

Donna was soft where Rachel was hard. My hands kept pausing as the flesh gave way.

"I'm glad about what you're doing. I'm glad you're helping Mervyn." Her voice was as soft as her body. "They came into the gallery again today, those men. I told them you were down in the cellar working. Said you'd been working every day. Hard. They said they knew you were the sort of person they could do business with."

Donna seemed to be all flesh. My fingers never touched a bone at all.

"Bill," I said.

"We haven't made love for years. He goes to see some French tart in North Oxford every weekend. Come in, Tom. It's not like it was that time."

"Tom," she said, over and over again as I tried to disappear inside her. A brief oblivion. Soon enough the nerves started to pull tight again.

It can't have been much after dawn that I woke, Donna sprawled out beside me. That mop of blond hair, her breasts so heavy against the mattress. I crept out of bed, put my clothes on, and left.

When I arrived at the flat in Paddington there was a letter on the floor. From Oxford.

My dear Tom,
You have made your decision, the wrong one, but who am I to tell you anything?

How easily you are led, Tom. I suppose men whose mothers were holes that they fell into are easily led. Some women are all rats and snakes behind their smiles. The bigger the smile the more rats and snakes.

Now you are pretending again, I suppose, pretending you are someone who is dead. I could never touch you again if you are doing that. I don't want a corpse in my bed. Don't come.

I wonder sometimes if you'll ever understand anything—about yourself or others.

This world's not here to say yes to.

I love you,
Rachel.

I read the letter over and over again. I read it in the flat and then in the different pubs I sat in that day. Rachel. She had said I didn't love anyone and maybe she was right, but if I loved anyone at all, it was her. And that was why those men weren't going to come after her, whatever I had to do to stop them.

22

Dark

All places shall be hell that is not heaven.
C H R I S T O P H E R   M A R L O W E , *Doctor Faustus*

*Delaquay's Diary. June 11, 1900. Delaquay Proceedings, Volume
Thirteen.*

*The interchangeability of bodies. Once Don Juan has started on his
journey it makes no difference which body is which. This is purely
a matter of erotic statistics. This is all sexual data. One piece of
flesh softer or paler than the last is not a matter for remark. God
absents himself with ever-greater frequency from each carcass.*

*Baudelaire understood this. The body approaches more and
more the state of the inanimate. Its groans and sighs, its heaving
and its sweat, signify only mechanical movement. Don Juan wishes
to have ecstatic union with a soul. It is a sacrament he craves.*

*My unions with prostitutes are at least conducted under the
sacramental aegis of cash, the true divinity of our time. We have
at least told the Satan of hypocrisy to get behind us. Like Danaë's
gash, the wound is filled with gold.*

*Intoxication or death, the only choices. The same choice, I
suppose. Unless I repent.*

I went back there and worked. I could hardly bring myself to talk to
Donna.

"You don't have to feel guilty," she said.

"Don't I?"

"People get lonely."

"Try Soho," I said. "It's full of lonely people. You could make a living down there. Bill wouldn't mind, I'm sure. He could do the limericks for you."

She was wearing a miniskirt. A little young for her, it seemed to me.

"I'll be downstairs," I said. "Working. No interruptions. We do want your brother to heal up nicely and get all his debts paid, don't we?"

Driven, obsessional, ferocious work. I hadn't thought it possible to draw so much. I didn't even have to think as I did it. My hand had a mind of its own. Faustus. This was all clocks and sundials and evening shadows. Everywhere that Faustus looks he sees the passage of time that must destroy him. He tries to build his earthly paradise from the exercise of power, but he can see hell behind it every minute as the calendar shifts toward his settlement.

I used what I could remember of necromantic signs and symbols from my reading of the Proceedings. I had the Doctor in his circle summoning the spirits, as Delaquay himself claimed to have done three hundred years later in Paris. One of the spirits that hovered about him I made into Delaquay's succubus. I gave her Donna's body. I was finished by the end of the week. Exhausted and empty. I didn't know who I was anymore, and I didn't care either.

I was drinking straight whiskey and flicking through them when Mervyn came down. He didn't look too bad. His face had reset at an angle, but this made it more interesting. He seemed to squint at you now, as though he were actually interested in finding out who you were.

"Well done, Tom. I knew you wouldn't let us down."

"I'd like a hundred pounds, Mervyn. Then I'd like to get out of this place for a while. You will let me know, won't you, if anything's left over after you've paid off your friends? We were going fifty-fifty, remember?"

"I remember. Where are you going tonight?"

"Oh, a meal at the Ritz, take in a show at the West End, perhaps the opera, the usual."

"Let me buy you dinner at Luigi's. Then later on we'll go to the Billet. Always meant to take you there."

I didn't decide to go with Mervyn. I simply didn't have the strength to decide not to. There were no decisions left in me. Donna joined us for dinner then left to reacquaint herself with the other Tom.

"Glad you two are getting on so well," Mervyn said.

Luigi was solicitous.

"How it happen?"

"Fell down the cellar stairs in the gallery, Luigi. I was drunk, I'm afraid."

"Could happen to anyone."

"Actually, Luigi," I said, leaning across the table, "two men he owed a lot of money to came and beat him up."

"Ah yes, bad men from Sicily," Luigi said, and laughed.

"The police would probably have the same amount of interest if you ever decided to go and talk to them," Mervyn said. He smiled his all-purpose smile. The deformation of his expression as the stitches pulled upward had undoubtedly improved it. When dinner was finished we walked to the Billet.

Halfway along Dean Street there was a seedy-looking staircase of the sort I'd often made my way up, after hearing an invitation from inside. At the top of this, through an unmarked door, was what looked like the rudimentary stage set for a bar. The place was already half full and Bella was sitting on her stool smoking. Long black hair fell to her shoulders. She wore a strapless cocktail dress and looked as though she might start singing at any moment. Bella, I soon discovered, was our hostess. She obviously knew Mervyn well and was delighted at the recent rearrangement of his features.

"So you finally decided to take our advice and have that face-lift done," she cackled merrily. "You do look better. Peter, come over here and look at our new member."

A man with short gray hair and eyes as blue and piercing as Grimshaw's came over and stared intently at Mervyn's features.

"You look almost human, Astley," he said. "The proof for the skeptics that evolution's possible."

"Well, thank you, Peter," Mervyn said. "Let me introduce my partner, Tom Lynch. Tom, this is the painter Peter Quetzel, whom I once had the privilege to represent."

"Yes, until I decided it would be nice to actually get *paid* something. Happy memories, eh, Mervyn?"

"Well, come on, my little rodent," Bella said, "do tell us who did your makeup for you."

"It was a misunderstanding," Mervyn said.

"Yours, by the look of it," Peter said. "Didn't realize that this time you weren't dealing with people who only had brushes in their pockets."

"Could we have a bottle of champagne, please, Bella," Mervyn said, reasserting his smile. "We're celebrating."

"Your father can't have died again, Mervyn."

"No. We will shortly be announcing another Delaquay exhibition. Which, after the success of the last one . . ."

"Where's it all coming from, Mervyn?" Peter asked. "For years no one's allowed to own any of this stuff unless they have a special operation and shake hands under their legs, now suddenly you have lorry loads of it turning up every weekend."

"Sources in Paris," Mervyn said. Conspiratorial. Professional.

"Oh, sources in Paris," Bella cried, with a whoop.

"Well, bugger me, sweetheart, sources in Paris. What can a chap say? Always were rather saucy, the French. And what do you do?" Peter said, looking at me with unnerving precision.

"Same as him," I said, taking my champagne from Mervyn.

"That one so young should so lack all belief!"

Mervyn left after a while. He didn't seem entirely comfortable. No one was sorry to see him go.

"Your partner is a git," Peter said.

"Couldn't agree more," I said.

This seemed to cheer him somewhat. "Then why . . . ?"

"Money," I said. "But not for long."

"Good," he said. I offered him some of the champagne from the bottle that was left.

"No," he said, "I'm afraid I don't."

There came from the direction of the bar a piercing female voice I'd not heard before. "Which of these inadequates is going to end up frigging me tonight?"

"Ah," Peter said sadly. "Sonia Lavery has arrived. Sweet, shy, mysterious creature. Daddy owns half of the west coast of Scotland, don't you know, so Sonia proves it has nothing to do with her by whoring it up with the Bohemians. A profoundly tiresome woman, though I'm told her body is not to be underestimated.

"Come and see me if you like. Here's my address. That's my studio. Work there every day. Always happy to have a little company. I can't fit you into my brain with Mervyn at all. Someone, I fear, has made a pairing mistake. Oh Sonia, how lovely to see you. Still as reticent as ever, I see. Left to blush unseen and all that. Let me introduce you to Tom Lynch, the partner—believe it or not—of Mervyn Astley."

Sonia looked me over with frank appraisal. "I like them small now and then," she said. "Makes a change from some of the brutes I get."

I didn't decide to go back with Sonia in the early hours of that morning either. When I had decided not to go back to Rachel but to stay in London and start impersonating Delaquay again, that decision took all the strength out of me. I couldn't decide anything anymore after that. It was as though I had made my last decision.

I didn't even like Sonia. She was certainly the loudest lover I had ever been with. As she shouted out instructions and responses, I found myself wondering if she had ever had any neighbors. When she finally fell asleep, she snored. I didn't sleep myself until dawn. When I woke up she was gone. There was a note on the table.

Lovely evening. Thank you. Please set latch as you leave.
Which of the seven are you, by the way?
Snow White.

I came out blurred into the street. Which street? I walked through the tunnel of my hangover until I recognized my surroundings. Dean Street again. Was the Billet open? The Billet, I was soon to discover, was always open. Calling at an inopportune moment might bring down a thousand curses from Bella on your head, but you would never be turned away.

"Gin, I think," I said after some reflection. "A double gin with a single tonic."

"Good night with the virgin of Skye?"

"No. I suspect a very bad one."

"Same thing, my sweet. When you're my age you'll realize that they're one and the same thing."

There was a skirmish of pain down the left side of my skull which I was trying to aim the gin at. There was a very slight numbing all over as the drink started to bite. Something about gin in a glass and the way the ice tinkles against it. I sipped and tinkled. I felt glad that I was welcome in this place. I lifted up the glass toward Bella and tinkled it.

"Goat bells on a Sicilian hill," I said.

Bella eyed me with grave skepticism and poured herself a substantial whiskey.

"Sheep's piss in a Scottish loch," she said, and chimed her glass against mine before downing the lot in one.

I started to go there every day. I had to go back to Mervyn once or twice for more money. I told him I didn't want to have anything to do with the exhibition. This didn't seem to bother him. He even said he knew now how to write the catalog himself.

"As long as you sign it," he said, handing me the money.

They came and went, Bella's strange clientele.

One Friday morning I meandered my way across Soho, carrying the burden of last night in my skull, my gut, and my liver. The woman shushed out from a doorway and was weaving in front of me before I could avoid her. Her hair was matted and the whole right side of her face bejeweled with dark red scabs. Plenty of fatty tissue had been torn up there, either by an argumentative flight of stairs or her latest boyfriend. Did she fall or was she pushed? I wasn't going to ask because I didn't care. But those beseeching eyes, almost weeping with the acid afterbirth of drink. I could have done without that beseeching. I had clamors enough of my own inside.

"Juz the prize of a coffee," she said. Her hand reached out toward me and I could smell her. What was it? Sherry? Meths? I put my hand into my pocket and pulled out the first coins my fingers closed around. They disappeared into the bruise of her hand, her fingers enormous for some reason, mottled Lincoln sausages black-tipped with nails. I caught the whiff of her urinous clothes now.

At the Billet serious drinkers were recouping their losses from the night before. They hunched over the bar with scholarly concentration on the glass before them. I joined them. Double gin. Half tonic.

"You look bad," Bella said, fixing me with that stare of hers as she breathed out the cigarette smoke.

"It's the drink," I said.

"I know what it is," she said. "I've seen plenty on the chute you're sliding down. How do you actually make a living, Tom, in here every day?"

"From my interest in the Astley Gallery," I said.

"Yes, I can see that would be enough to keep anyone's tongue in the bottle. You should eat, though. When was the last time you ate?"

"I can't remember."

"I'll make you some sandwiches."

I hadn't even noticed him come in, let alone slide onto the bar stool beside me, but as the hand slicked back and forth for his glass, I saw that the crimson bracelets went all the way up to his elbow, some cut with surgical precision, others hacked at, as though one hand had risen in a frenzy against the other. He saw me studying his arm.

"If thy right hand offend thee, cut it off." He rolled his shirtsleeve down again. "Believe every word of the Bible myself."

I wanted to ask him if one hand knew what the other was doing: he was pouring white wine from his bottle into my gin. I turned around cautiously to look at him. He had the look of a discredited policeman or a cashiered junior officer. Short back and sides while all around were growing theirs. Either he was working on a beard for his incognito or his diary was presently too full to get together with a razor blade.

"Demons," he said, "all the demons of hell behind the glass there. Invisible spirits creep in at the crushing of the grapes." The voice low and compelling. "Little grape demons. Vicious little sods. Want everyone in hell, paying Lucifer's mortgage."

"Why do you drink it, then, my precious?" Bella asked, putting my sandwiches on the bar. He started to eat them straight away.

"Enough of this inside me and I'll smash some place to bits and get banged up again by the filth."

"Not my place, you won't. You go round to someone else's bar to be a silly boy." Bella's voice was seductive but anxious.

"I've never done anything in here," he said. Then in a movement of impressive fluency he was over the bar, holding Bella hard by both shoulders. He was shouting now. "Why do you think I come here? It's not the drink—I can get this piss cheaper in plenty of other places. It's certainly not the conversation, is it?" As he said this he turned toward me and started laughing. "It's you, Bella, it's your body that I lusted over all those nights in the nick. It's the haughty profile of your face. It's the strawberry rush of your nipples."

By now Bella was laughing. Everyone in the bar relaxed and shifted back into ironic mode.

"You are a silly boy, you know. Get over that bar and drink quietly."

He stood at the side of me again and ate the sandwiches. When he had finished them he took hold of my right ear and brought my face within an inch of his own.

"And if thine eye offend thee, pluck it out. For it is better to enter blind the kingdom of heaven than to burn in hell fire."

His breath smelled bad.

"I must leave you, Bella. The wine in this establishment is unsanctified and quenches nothing."

A minute later he was gone.

"Very talented, actually," Bella confided. "Did a wonderful portrait of me once. Nude. Still have it upstairs." Her eyes swung momentarily heavenward. I stayed there drinking till the place started to go dim in the dusk.

23

Aflame

The whore's old clients smile
Drained of misery awhile;
My arms beseech but fail
That wrapped themselves round clouds.

Thanks to the stars so nonpareil
Torching the remotest sky
I see nothing but bright lights gone
Through blind mementos of the sun.

For nothing it seems I sought out
The vacuum that is space's heart;
Under the enigma of the fire's eye
My wax melts, my feathers fly

And charred by love of what I crave
I'll not even have the pleasure
Of naming at last the shifting grave
Where my bones dump their treasure.

CHARLES BAUDELAIRE, "Icarus's Cries"

Delaquay's Diary. August 1901. Delaquay Proceedings, Volume
Fourteen.

You must not fear Sheol. Must not fear Acheron. Must not fear
Hades. I had to make this whole journey to come to understand

that. Here amidst the darkness and light of the streets of Paris. Mustn't fear those flames. They blister away skin you've stayed hidden in. Burn you to brightness. Furnaces working day and night to restore you. Are there fires in Sheol? Then they'll melt down your sorrows along with your sins. Be a torch then, be a beacon, a light to yourself and to others. Purging, cleansing, fires not measured in time. No tears douse them. Learn how to welcome what burns you. That's all.

■

I hadn't really slept, merely twitched in and out of oblivion all night. When I woke my skin itched all over with leprous intensity. A knife was stabbing the back of my eyes. My tongue felt like dried suede. But, then, I felt like this most of the time now.

I was checking in my coat to see what money I might have left when the card fell out. Peter Quetzel. My first night at the Billet. I set off immediately to see him. Couldn't tell you why.

There is a terrace of houses along the Talgarth Road with enormous windows. They were built by a philanthropist so that artists might have the light they needed when working. Peter lived in one of these. I pressed the bell. He was wearing loose old clothes covered with paint. He smiled.

"Tom, I'd given up on you. Come in."

I followed him up to his studio. Inside was a wonderful chaos of paints and brushes, sheets and canvases.

"Sit anywhere you think it might be possible," he said. He looked at me carefully. "Are you all right?"

"No. I'm not. You wouldn't have anything to drink, would you?"

"You mean seriously to drink? There might be some sherry in the kitchen, but that would be it. I don't, you see, not anymore. There's an off-license round the corner . . ."

I had stood up again. Then I had to turn back.

"You couldn't lend me some money, could you? It's just I don't seem to have brought any with me."

"Don't worry," he said. "I know what it's like to have to work with Mervyn Astley. I did it myself once, you know."

He handed me a note from his wallet. I bought a bottle of gin and some tonic.

I was sitting back in his studio, sipping it with a rumor of well-being starting somewhere toward the back of my head.

"We have something in common, Tom," Peter said as he daubed some background color onto his canvas. "We're both alcoholics. It's just I'm an alcoholic who doesn't drink and you're an alcoholic who does."

I'd not had that word applied to me before. It felt clinical and offensive.

"I'm not an alcoholic," I said. "I've just been drinking a lot lately. I've had some bad—"

"No, take it from me, you're an alcoholic. No more reason to be ashamed of it than there is to be proud of it. Just the way you are. Filling up some hole inside. Somebody once dug a hole in you. You might even have dug it yourself. Either way, it makes no difference. The hole's there. The hole may well be the most interesting thing about you. Often is. Most alcoholics I know are of above-average intelligence and even sensitivity. The real question is, how much longer can you go on feeling so bloody awful? Maybe it's until the day you die. I know people who've done that. For myself I decided I had some work to do. It wasn't easy. It's never easy. But I knew I must either climb out of the poisonous river or drown. Do you have any work to do, Tom? Right now, if I had to ascribe a provenance, I'd say *School of Mervyn Astley, 1966.* All the way down to the bottom."

"How do I stop?" I said.

"You just stop," he said as he painted. "You can go into a hospital to do it. Or stay at home and chew the carpet. You can even stay here if you like. But you either keep on or stop. Trouble is, in my experience, nobody ever stops unless it's got so bad that something inside them really needs the change. I'm not sure with you."

"Do you mind if I have some more gin and think about it?" I said.

"Not at all. You must understand, there's nothing judgmental in anything I say. I merely make observations."

I had made my way round his canvas. He was painting mostly in black. It was some kind of hybrid, some great black shaggy underground creature.

"The Minotaur," he said. "Part of a sequence I'm doing. You wouldn't pose for me, would you? You're just the right size for Icarus."

I kept going round there each day. I switched from gin to white wine and started to calm down a little. It didn't bother me taking my clothes off in front of Peter. I often talked as he painted. Once, he came over and put his hand on my leg as he moved it to the position he wanted.

"Not queer at all, then?" he said.

"Don't think so."

"Pity," he said. "Let me know if you ever feel like trying it out. *I've* been with women, you know."

"Why this particular myth?" I asked him.

"Maybe I'm a sun worshiper," he said. "It appeals to me, I suppose. It seems to say that we can't cope either with too much light or too much darkness. The Minotaur is hidden away in the dark, the product of shame. Miscegenation. Daedalus builds the place of darkness. Then he has to devise a means of escaping it himself. Wings. Wings for himself and his son. But the son goes too near the light and finds his own death. Maybe that's what he has to find. No father can stop a son doing that if that's the nature of his search.

"Then the Minotaur. I don't believe those stories about him feeding on young men and women. My instincts tell me that the young men and women were probably the misshapen ones, the ones with twisted tongues and unacceptable dreams. I think he protected them when they cast them in there, into the labyrinth, so that their families didn't have to look on the shame of their difference.

"I also think Icarus is the spirit of Daedalus without the cunning. That's why he flies too near the sun. That's why he dies. We all love the reckless, even if we can't follow them. You must be getting cold, Tom. Put your clothes back on. Pour yourself another drink. And this time drink it very slowly."

One morning I turned up there and he tossed a copy of the *Evening News* across to me.

"You and your partner must be feeling pretty pleased with yourselves."

The Delaquay exhibition had been reviewed. "Brilliant," "an astonishing series of discoveries," "opens a whole new door onto the genius of *fin-de-siècle* Paris."

"I did them," I said.

Peter looked at me for a moment, saying nothing.

"All of them?"

"Yes. And the ones before."

"Good God! Why?"

"I don't know. That's the way it all turned out. It's hard to explain. All sorts of reasons . . . I'm going to buy some drink."

"I thought you'd promised yourself not to anymore in the mornings."

"You know all about alcoholic promises."

"Sadly, I do."

I opened the gin and started to talk. Peter carried on working but from time to time he looked across at me and whistled. When I'd finished he started laughing.

"Tom, that's the most extraordinary story I've ever heard. It's obviously true. Nobody would make up anything so entirely pointless."

This last word was not intended cruelly but the sharpened point of it stuck into me. Pointless. I poured half a glass of gin and gulped it. Pointless.

"I'm sorry, I didn't mean to hurt you, Tom. But you must face it, surely? Unless you face up to the sheer bloody pointlessness of it, where can you go?"

"I don't know where to go anyway."

"But I saw some of those drawings. They were remarkably skillful. If you can do that, why can't you do something of your own?"

"Never could. Don't know why. But I could never do anything out of myself."

"Maybe that's because you were telling lies. To yourself, admittedly, but then those are the worst ones of all. Here. Look. Come over here now."

He pulled the canvas he was working on from the easel and put a fresh one there.

"Come on. Paint me. What's the matter? What are you, frightened of? Paint me. What do you want? What color?"

"Black," I said.

So I fumbled and muttered as he sat there staring at me, but I went on, and as I went on I started to find something there, some shape that was his head and his face. Amidst the mangle of my own self-doubt something was starting to emerge. He looked at it when I had finished.

"Certainly not Delaquay," he said.

"No."

"And yet, it might be more intriguing, you know, precisely because it's so . . . incompetent, I suppose. There's something alive in it. Those Delaquays—or should I say Lynches?—all sealed up. Perfected. There's something here . . . I don't know. . . . It's pretty shaky, though. A little sodden-looking."

"Drink."

"Afraid so. If you could give it up, you might do something interesting, but I doubt very much you'd ever make a living out of it. Not that I do most of the time, come to that."

"I'll be here tomorrow morning sober," I said.

Peter kissed me gently on the forehead. "Good man," he said.

When I arrived back at the flat that afternoon, the solicitor's letter was waiting. I had to read it three times before I realized what had happened. When Agatha died Grimshaw had obviously decided not to tell me. I suppose he was simply so disgusted at what I had done that he couldn't bring himself to contact me at all. But anyone could have predicted that he himself would not outlive her for long. Now they were both gone.

The solicitor requested my presence the following Tuesday in his offices in Ilkley. I must have knelt on the floor for ten minutes staring at that letter before I finally got to my feet again.

Mervyn was in a celebratory mood at the gallery. Donna had a new coiffure and the cut of her dress was designed to make a feature of her breasts.

"Here's the wonderboy himself," Mervyn said. "We had been wondering when we would see you again. We need to make some serious plans."

"I need some money, Mervyn."

"And you shall have it," he said. Donna was glowing at me. "We've done very well indeed, I can tell you. We are now attracting the foreign buyers. Delaquay is on the map."

"I want two hundred pounds, then you can forget about me."

"Forget about you? My dear chap, this is no time to be forgetting about one another. You don't seem to realize the little pot of gold we've landed on. Two hundred pounds is far too little. Have a thousand. I have a list of titles here—"

"Two hundred will do."

"Don't have it in cash."

"Go and get it, then."

He went out. I walked around the gallery. There were far more pink circles than blue ones on the frames. I noticed he had increased the price to five hundred pounds each.

"How's Bill?" I said.

"So-so."

"And your son?"

"Lovely. A real treasure."

"Tell your brother that it's all over, will you? Just tell him, I'm finished."

She looked at me with genuine alarm. When Mervyn walked in with the money, I took it and left while he was in midsentence.

In the hotel above the Cow and Calf I stared through the window at those rocks. I was in the same room where I had stayed with Rachel. Sobriety hurt. I went downstairs to the bar.

"Could I have a large whiskey, please?"

"Certainly, sir. In this weather, I think we all need one."

Later I drove down to the village and bought a bottle. No food all day. I woke at dawn nauseous and threw up in the toilet. I missed breakfast and drove to Bolton Abbey by nine. I had my sketchbook with me. I started work on some of the fragments of tracery. Peter was right. My line was shaky and my style nondescript. My hand didn't know who it belonged to.

I walked into the pub at twelve. A pint of Tetley's. Rachel had liked Tetley's. We had come here together. I ordered a cheese salad but couldn't eat it.

When I arrived at the solicitor's office the next day he was cold, methodical. I thought I sensed an element of distaste in his gestures and demeanor.

"The house and all its contents together with all the savings of Patrick Grimshaw are left in their entirety to Thomas Lynch. All the policies and savings when redeemed will come to approximately ten thousand pounds. The valuation of the house and its contents you must ascertain for yourself.

"Would you care for a sherry, sir?" he asked.

"You wouldn't have anything stronger?"

"I could ask Miss Jenkins to fetch you a Scotch, if that would be preferable."

"It would."

"With or without water?"

"Without."

"There is a somewhat unusual codicil to this will. In fact, I think I'm right in saying, a unique codicil. It is requested of you that you sign the enclosed document. If you refuse to do so, then all the aforementioned bequests are rescinded."

"What is the document?"

"I'll read it to you:

"I hereby agree to assisting in every way possible with the retro-spective exhibition of the work of Alfred Delaquay to be arranged next year by the Archivist in New York. The exhibition will be held in London at a venue to be specified. I agree to submitting all works ascribed to Delaquay, including those in the Grimshaw home in Ilkley, and all works exhibited under the name of Delaquay at the Astley Modern Gallery in London. I will do everything in my power to place every work in any way associated with Delaquay in this exhibition."

I signed it.

"Where are they buried?" I asked.

"The little churchyard on the Skipton Road. You know it?"

"Yes," I said. "Grimshaw took me there when I was a boy."

Before I left his office he gave me a set of keys. "The house of Patrick and Agatha," he said. "Yours now." I drove over to the graveyard. Next to one another, two new headstones. All the stones around them were worn and lichened. My eyes were blurred with the cold wind. But I looked hard anyway. Even knelt to look. And stared for a long time before I actually saw.

Patrick Grimshaw

Beloved Husband
of
Agatha

Father of Thomas

24

Landing

It was once thought that fire was an element. But fire is a process in which the elements intermarry, so that matter is renewed and the hands of man grow warm. It is only the mind, in the rigidity of its presuppositions, which melts.
ISAAC LENAU, *Marginalia*, 909

I WALKED AROUND THE HOUSE. I SAT ON THE NARROW BED I'D once slept in. I looked at all those little framed Delaquays hanging on the walls. On the table was an envelope. On the outside it simply said *Tom.*

My dear boy,

Since you are reading this, I am dead. And since I am dead there seems little point in trying to keep anything further from you.

You may already have realized by now that Agatha was my wife. And you may be shrewd enough to have realized that we had a son. Our son was your father.

This has the air about it of one of the less successful Jacobean dramas, I know, but there is nothing to be done now. I do not intend to attempt to justify anything to you. We must all leave the justification to God in any case.

If I say that I was once in training to be a priest and that Agatha once lived in a convent, perhaps you may piece together all the other little bits of the jigsaw without my numbering them for you.

Your father was put out for adoption. It seemed unavoidable at the time though like most unavoidable things it could have been avoided. Your grandmother and I subsequently married. It seemed cruel by then to wrench your father away. Even for me to retain a job in Catholic education, let alone become headmaster of Southwell, required some subterfuge. We became brother and sister. Well, for the purposes of the world we did.

I wish I could enlighten you more about your father, but I cannot. That is not for me to do. All will become clear, I think, in the next year.

Agatha and I were greatly saddened to hear that your plans for a marriage with Rachel were going into abeyance. We had a strange match ourselves, but came to understand one thing out of it all. If two people love each other with honesty and conviction, all the institutional disapproval that surrounds them is so much dross.

Perhaps the breach between you is not irreparable.

I leave you by telling you posthumously what I could never properly tell you while I was alive.

Which is to say, how much I and your grandmother loved you. More than either of us could ever say.

May God bless you,
Patrick

Grimshaw always kept half a bottle of everything in his little cupboard. It never seemed to change from year to year. I suppose they never drank any of it. Sure enough, there was half a bottle of Scotch there. As I drank my way through it, I decided that Grimshaw's blessing was in a way an instruction.

At eleven o'clock that night I set off in the Jaguar. I was a little unsteady but knew that as the night wore on I'd sober up. I'd be outside Rachel's flat by dawn.

I think the tears in my eyes were tears of recognition. I was beginning to understand who I was. I had to swerve as I nearly went off the road and slowed the car to eighty. Hardly any other people driving though—it was safe enough in that regard. Anyway, I'd driven when I was a lot drunker than this and I'd never hit anything yet.

I tried to make out as much of the landscape as I could in the dark. When the moon came clear of the clouds I could see the hills. We'd walk them again, Rachel and I. I wanted to cover all the ground with her that Grimshaw had covered with me. That would be my act of remembrance to him.

My foot seemed to sink slowly into the accelerator. I was powering along a wide, straight, sleepy carriageway until the bend appeared from nowhere. Then suddenly the embankment was underneath my nearside wheel and as I tried to turn the car back to the road, it simply lifted off from the top of the little hill. A million lights all smeared their way over the windscreen, though I didn't know where they'd come from. Then the clatter of the ground ceased. That moment in the air was strangely serene. I was flying. When the car hit the concrete support at the bottom I was thrown through the windscreen and I heard a sound around me like screaming and then there was nothing at all.

■

The next thing I remember is St. Anthony's Hospital, South Yorkshire. I could just see through the bandages. There were plasters on my arms and legs and heavy bandages around my ribs. It was hard to breathe. My face felt as though all the skin had been flayed away.

"Lucky to be alive at all," the nurses kept saying.

They asked me if there was anyone who should be notified. They had not been able to find anyone from my records. The only person I could think of was Peter. I gave them his address.

Two days later he arrived.

"You should have got the train, Tom," he said, smiling, but through my bandages I could see how shaken he was.

"The coppers would have done you for drunken driving, but

they were so convinced you'd die they didn't bother making out the reports."

I began to wonder what I was going to look like at the end of all this.

I found out six weeks later.

I don't think it's possible to explain to anyone else how it is to look suddenly like a different human being. Most people do it stage by stage, inch by inch. The skin creases up, the hair falls out, the blood vessels burst. But I looked in the mirror and saw a piece of crazy paving where my face had been.

"It will gradually settle," the doctor said, without much conviction. "It's all still very angry now around the cuts. We could try plastic surgery later, if you feel you can't live with it. Wasn't possible at this stage. It's partly up to you. We managed to get most things functioning again. Though not up to full capacity.

"When you came in here, you were about eighty percent proof. If you start drinking again, there's things down there won't last long, frankly. We can only do so much. A lot was ruptured and split. You're lucky to be alive at all, you must understand that."

I stood and stared into the mirror. It wasn't me there. Some old man, some veteran of the trenches. I wondered if it might not have been a wiser move simply to die. When people start to tell you often enough that you're lucky to be alive, it's probably themselves they're trying to convince.

Peter took me back to his house on the train.

"At least it got me off the bottle, Peter," I said, as we came into King's Cross.

"I could have shown you some easier ways," he said.

"Like what?"

"Oh, filling in your mouth with concrete and cutting off your fingers. Old Sicilian cure for drinking. Though sometimes they still cheat and suck it up their noses with a straw."

"I've reached the bottom of it," I said, turning my zigzag of a face toward him.

"You'll be all right," he said. He didn't look as though he believed it. I didn't believe it either.

Peter was painting and I was in the armchair he'd moved over to the window for me when Solomon Levine first arrived. Tall, thin, dark-jowled, with big thick glasses that he seemed to look through desperately as though he was lost, he was carrying a small pile of magazines. Badly printed on cheap paper.

"I have the latest *Kafka's Ledger,* Peter," he said. "How many could you take?"

"Four," Peter said, without stopping painting. "Meet Tom Lynch. Artist. Invalid. Dipso. Dried-out. Lodger. I painted him as Icarus, then he went and prepared himself for the next picture: Icarus after the fall. Never come across such devotion in a model before."

Solly came over and smiled at me. "Would you like one?"

"What is it?"

"My journal. *Kafka's Ledger.*"

"It's devoted to translation," Peter said as he painted. "But only three people ever get translated in it. Who are they again, Sol?"

"Kafka, Mandelstam, and Celan," Solly said.

"Why those?"

"German and Russian are my languages. And I can only translate people who struggle for breath on the page."

"Solly leaves blanks for the bits he can't do," Peter said.

"I only translate what I can translate," he said. "Translation is theft anyway."

"Tom knows all about theft," Peter said. "He worked for years with Mervyn Astley."

When I finally made it to the gallery, Donna was there. She kept looking down toward the desk as she spoke, and shuffling papers.

"So nice to see you again, Tom. You're obviously recovering well.

I'm sure Mervyn would be delighted to have a word. He talks about you all the time. He's out at the framers at the moment, I'm afraid."

"I need the keys to the safe, Donna."

"Well, I couldn't give you those. As you know. Mervyn—"

"Give me the keys, Donna, or I'll write an article for the *Evening News* about the last Delaquay exhibition."

I made it down the steps without too much trouble. It was becoming easier to walk all the time. I just kept the stick as a balance. I opened up the safe. I took out the Milton and the Baudelaire. I was about to close it again, when I decided Mervyn owed me a lot more than I owed him. I took the Dante too. None of my early drawings were in there. He must have put them somewhere else. I didn't care anymore.

As I left I waved the books in the air at Donna.

"My payment. Let Mervyn know, would you? The account between us is settled, but he'll be called on to exhibit soon."

"Exhibit what?"

"All the Delaquays that have passed through his hands. All the ones whose provenance traces back through this gallery. It will seem a little odd if he doesn't—what with all the others being there."

25

Kafka's Ledger

*All poetry is protest. All poetry protests against the Tower of
Babel. This is what Mandelstam meant by saying that Acmeism
was a nostalgia for world culture. All poems aspire to be
translated before they are even written, translated into every
language, or one true one. The language of the poem is so
uniquely rich precisely to remind us of what we are deaf and
blind to, as this massive century we've constructed comes
crashing round our ears.*
SOLOMON LEVINE, Editorial, *Kafka's Ledger*

PETER HAD ALL THE BACK COPIES OF SOLLY'S JOURNAL. MORE
and more I found myself reading them.

"Intriguing, isn't it?" Peter said.

"Never come across anything like it."

"Does it all himself. Everything. And every line of translation . . . the
lines he does, that is. There's a great purity about Solly. Makes one fear
for him.

"Do you mind doing it again?"

"What?" I said.

"Posing."

"Naked?"

"Yes."

"You're sure you want to see?"

"I've seen worse."

"Don't count on it."

Peter helped me out of my clothes. I had to lean against a chair to keep myself balanced.

"Really did leave that car with a bang, didn't you?"

"Changed your mind, have you?"

"About what?"

"Your previous proposition?"

"No," he said unsteadily. He had, though, and we both knew it. Somewhere in Soho there was probably a lady who specialized in cripples with mangled faces, but I didn't feel I had the energy to seek her out. He was playing Dylan on his gramophone.

"I wouldn't have thought he was your sort of thing, Peter."

"He has his own song. Not many people ever find that."

Solly would come round and talk to me. As my legs became stronger we would walk down to the river together. Sometimes he would go in to buy himself a pint. I stayed outside and drank nothing. When an alcoholic stops drinking he loses the skin that had protected him from everything he flees. Now there is only the raw, tender flesh of his mind, and the memories he can no longer drown. I sensed that Solly was drawn to me for the same reasons that others were driven away. Sometimes he would turn up with a dark-haired woman, who would say little but fidgeted distractedly with the buttons on her jacket. She seemed always cross with Solly, as he went on obsessively. And he did go on obsessively. The bombing, as he called it. You couldn't escape Vietnam by that stage. The newspapers, the radio, the television, theater, the street demonstrations, and all those songs, most of them terrible.

But Solly was obsessed with the language of it, with the management of it all in words. "They had to destroy the village in order to save it," he said. "And don't you ever doubt that they'll destroy the rest of us too in order to save us if that's what it comes to."

"Who are *they,* Solly?"

"The misusers of language," he said, "the builders of the latest modernity. People in high places, or lower ones for that matter, who destroy villages in order to save them. People who can calculate the precise amount of overkill required so we have the same capacity to wipe out all human life on the earth as many times over as the other side. Life itself dies in this language. The same life that Celan and Mandelstam had to fight for breath to keep."

I read all eight copies of *Kafka's Ledger* that Peter had, and I looked forward to Solly's intermittent visits. He didn't fit into any of the movements going on out there, I understood that. He dragged me along to a meeting on Vietnam in Victoria. His interventions were all unilateral, all pointing out the impossibility of some statement or other. One of the members of Mayday International finally turned on him in fury.

"Just what, Mr. Levine, would you say your politics are, exactly? Would you mind letting the rest of us in on the secret?"

Solly was grave and polite. "My politics are a language in which you can't bomb other people's children," he said.

"Then your language is one in which we couldn't have won the last war," came a voice from the back. "You'd have found plenty of little corpses in Dresden."

Solly left and I trailed out after him.

"You should never fill in someone else's silence with your own noise," he said to me.

Mandelstam fighting for breath through his verses, Kafka spitting up the word like blood from his tubercular lungs, Celan confronting in each book that death who was a master from Germany—these were Solly's subjects. Then one day he turned up at Peter's studio and announced that he was finished. There would be no more copies of *Kafka's Ledger.*

"Translation is a type of rape too," he said.

He didn't come back.

By then I was ready to move back into my own flat. I looked at Peter's finished picture.

"Why have you done the sun like that?" I said. "That circle with the black hole in the middle."

"First sign ever used as a symbol for hydrogen," he said. "John Dalton."

"Odd," I said. "Looks exactly like a cup and circle. And where did all the glass come from? I don't remember any glass in the story."

"That's the sky breaking as he falls through it," he said cheerfully. "Nice day. I'll walk up with you. Carry your bag. Keep those legs of yours moving."

26

Phoenix

Here the anthem doth commence:
Love and constancy is dead;
Phoenix and the Turtle fled
In a mutual flame from hence.
WILLIAM SHAKESPEARE,
"The Phoenix and the Turtle"

I WAS SITTING IN THE FLAT IN PADDINGTON TURNING OVER THE pages of the *Evening News* when I saw it.

ASTLEY GALLERY

announces

Further Works

from the
Delaquay Society.

Exhibition commences
NOVEMBER 1

The next day I set out walking. I had developed my own rolling gait that was quick enough, though a little inelegant. I kept the stick with me just in case, but I could move effectively through my chosen streets. I went to the Billet first. I wanted to say hello to Bella.

"My God, sweetie, who did you have an argument with?"

"Myself, I think."

"Have a drink."

"Could I have a glass of water?"

"I've never stocked that. Here, I'll give you a tonic without any gin. . . . Being a good boy now, are you?"

"No choice, Bella."

"That's the only way any of my boys get to be good, I'm afraid. It's always the same. Anyway, it's nice to see you. Makes a change from some of the riffraff I have to put up with around here." Her eyes scanned the bar. The men smiled back weakly.

I was on the point of leaving when Sonia Lavery arrived. She stopped in front of me and looked carefully at my face, then my legs, then my walking stick.

"Looks as though I had you just in time," she said. "Still got anything down there, have you?"

"Haven't looked," I said. "Nice to see some things in life don't change, Sonia. Age shall not wither you." I was shuffling across the floor but I could hear Bella's voice.

"You know, Sonia, it's not so much that you're an upper-class tart whose mouth is as big as her tits, it's more the fact that you are such a balls-aching . . ."

I stood looking through the window of the gallery. They were already putting up the pictures. My old pictures—the ones I had done in Oxford. Donna's face began to register some mild alarm as she recognized me. She said something. Mervyn appeared from the cellar. By this stage I was rolling through the door.

"Tom, how good to see you. You're obviously recovering well."

"Not even the right paper, Mervyn," I said, as I made my way around the walls. They were good, though. How could I ever have drawn like that? Now I fumbled and hesitated over the paper, now that I was finally trying to find some marks that might agree with the movements of my own mind. Those images on the wall weren't by me.

"It would be difficult to detect," he said. "I did some tests and it's debatable."

"I could put an end to all this, you know."

"You wouldn't do that."

"Wouldn't I?"

"There are outside interests still involved."

"Yes, I saw the Bentley outside. Yours, is it?"

"It's not new."

"You will send me a copy of the catalog, won't you?"

"Yes, indeed. Think you'll probably enjoy it. It's been written by Bill."
I looked at Donna. "Hasn't done it in limericks, has he?"

"We needed the money."

"I'm sure," I said.

"You won't be coming to the exhibition, then?" Mervyn asked.

"No. You can sleep easy in your bed on that score. I won't be at any more of *your* exhibitions."

"I'll split the money, of course," Mervyn said anxiously. "As we agreed."

"Keep the money, Mervyn," I said. "And I'll keep the Dante. That one's real."

The exhibition was a moderate success, though questions were starting to be asked about provenance. It was thought that the time had come for the Astley Gallery to be a little more forthcoming in regard to its Parisian sources. I sat and watched the television screen. Planes dropping bombs. Monks going up in flames. Students yelling at policemen on the streets.

The letter arrived one morning, postmarked New York.

Dear Tom,
You will remember that it was a condition of Patrick Grimshaw's will that you should collaborate in organizing an exhibition of all the known works of Alfred Delaquay.

We now intend to hold this exhibition in five months' time, in March of next year. It will be held at the Temple Gallery on the edge of Wimbledon Common. This may seem to some an unusual venue, but our requirements are not of the usual kind. The four separate internal rooms of that gallery will allow us to divide up the different aspects of Delaquay's work meaningfully.

You will arrange for the work of Delaquay held at the Grimshaws' house in Ilkley to be delivered a week before the first of March to the gallery. You will also deliver the books you are presently holding for display. The Oxford and New York Archives will deliver the rest.

We are anxious that this first full retrospective of Delaquay's work should be truly retrospective. For this reason we are making public announcements requesting that any work deemed to be by the artist should be offered for the exhibition. We would therefore be grateful if you could discuss with your collaborators at the Astley Gallery the methods of tracing all known holders of work ascribed to Delaquay which has been sold by them. We would expect any work held by the gallery itself to be on display too.

Sotheby's in London have agreed to make valuations of the work exhibited. Any work not forthcoming for the exhibition will be likely to have its provenance thrown into question.

I trust you are making a full recovery from your accident.

The Archivist
The Delaquay Society
New York.

■

I spent that Christmas alone in Ilkley.

"Why don't you come here, for God's sake?" Peter had said. "You're going to sit by yourself in a house of the dead on the edge of the Yorkshire moors in the middle of winter?"

Somehow I needed to go. I didn't need the walking stick anymore. I still walked with an odd shuffle but it wasn't so conspicuous now. My face had gradually calmed down. It was distinctively scarred but it didn't actually shout at passersby.

The house was cold. No one had lived in it for nearly a year. Peter was right, it was a house of the dead. That's why I was there. Perhaps all houses of memory are houses of the dead. I started to make an inventory of the Delaquays. One night, miserable and lonely, I opened up Grimshaw's drink cabinet. Just one to warm me.

I finished the sherry, the port, and the rum. The next day I was so ill I thought I'd die. I telephoned Peter and told him.

"Now you remember what it tastes like, don't you, before and after? Alcoholics shouldn't be alone at Christmas, I told you that."

My legs weren't strong enough to take me up to the Cow and Calf. I had to arrange a taxi, to the bemusement of the driver, who kept saying, "Is this all you want to do?"

"Yes," I said. "I just wanted to see it again. I'm not sure when I'll be back."

It was bleak and gray and icy. Sphinx's weather. I packed all the Delaquays carefully so that they'd be ready to ship down to London for the exhibition. Then I made arrangements about selling the house. There was no hurry. Grimshaw's will had left plenty of money in my bank.

I was back in London watching the television news. The camera was moving toward the porch of Westminster Abbey. A man had walked up briskly carrying a bag. He had sat down on the stones. He took from the bag a petrol can and poured the contents over his head, then the flames leapt as he flicked the lighter. His back was blazing and the fire was already eating away at his face. He was falling over onto his side, blazing away. And I knew who it was even before the voice-over began.

"A London translator, Solomon Levine, today set fire to himself before Westminster Abbey," the voice said, as the pictures showed people running toward him to throw their coats and jackets over the flames. "It is believed the protest was directed against the American war in Vietnam, in imitation of the protests of Buddhist monks. His condition is said to be critical."

I telephoned Peter.

"Ah, dear God, Sol," he said, as though to himself. "Dear Solly, what have you done, boy?"

It was months before we could see him. To begin with no one would even tell us where he was.

"He doesn't wish to be seen," the voices said.

Finally a little card arrived at Peter's house:

> Fire Escape
> Endleigh Nursing Home
> 48 The Esplanade
> Hove

We knew it was Solly. No one else was capable of such abbreviation. Peter and I went down together on the train. We walked along the seafront.

"Those legs have healed up well," Peter said.

"Yes, now all I need is a new face."

"You don't look that bad. I've been with sailors whose faces were a lot worse than that. And I was paying."

We sat and waited for a few minutes while the nurses went in and checked. His room was filled with disinfectant and the muslin curtains were drawn across the windows. His face was bandaged. The nurse left us.

"Quiet now," she said. "Don't get excited."

"Solly?"

"Hello, friends," he said, muffled in his gauze. "How's the painting going, Peter?"

"Oh, the canvases pile up, you know, waiting for that one patron of genuine discernment. We're still here, Sol. How much of you is?"

He unwound the bandage with great care. I had to look down for longer than I should have done before looking up again. The right eye was gone completely and a part of his nose too. All the hair and eyebrows and one ear. What was left was livid where the flame had tried to swallow it.

His left eye focused on us.

"So now you can see without the help of translation."

"What, Solly?"

"Truth. No adjectives. No adverbs. The lone noun."

27

Temple Gallery

If we accept that hell is fashioned out of the terrible depths of human experience, then we must logically conclude that hell is here among us now. I have nursed a shattered mind in the precincts of its temple, so I do not doubt it.
ISAAC LENAU, *Marginalia*, 24

I HAD SENT A COPY OF THE NEW YORK ARCHIVIST'S LETTER TO Mervyn.

He was shouting over the phone. "This is madness. You can't expect me to go along with this."

"Don't then, Mervyn," I said. "Explain to your customers and the press that you didn't want any of the Delaquays which you have handled to be in the retrospective. Then, perhaps, you'd be good enough to explain to them why."

There was a long silence while Mervyn pondered.

"Think of all those valuations, Mervyn, with the price increasing every day."

"It's not a proper gallery," he said.

"That's the one that's been chosen," I said.

"There'll have to be insurance cover."

"I'm not interested in any of that," I said. "All I have to do is make sure the work is there. If none of yours is, I'd have thought that it might look a little odd."

He was back on the phone half an hour later. "I've been phoning round. No insurance company will touch that gallery."

"So stay away," I said. "Keep your iffy Delaquays to yourself."

Mervyn was right. The Temple Gallery was made of wood, and it was a very strange venue for a major London exhibition. It stood on the edge of the Common, near to Wimbledon High Street. It had been put up in 1910 as an extensive Edwardian teahouse and now consisted of four large rooms. I looked at their back catalogs. Whatever else their exhibitions could be accused of, slavishly following fashion was not one of them. Their last showing had been Mongolian sacred instruments, the one before that eighteenth-century French embroidery.

"This is a new departure for us and we're very excited about it," Mrs. Simkins explained with her radiant smile. She must have been eighty. "I manage the gallery for the trust, you see. We're not used to receiving telephone calls from New York." Silver hair pulled back tightly, the way Agatha used to wear hers. Bright blue eyes. She'd been a real beauty once. Still was. "And then the purchase. Well, it came at a most opportune moment, I can tell you. We really had been struggling badly for a while. We'd have had to close."

"The purchase?"

"Yes. Didn't you know? The Delaquay Society has bought the gallery. It now belongs to them. They are exhibiting on their own premises."

We worked hard at the cataloging. Bill Blanchard turned up with a lorry filled with material from Oxford, including all the Proceedings.

He looked at me warily. "Got knocked about a bit, Tom?"

"I'm much recovered, thanks."

"I would have come to see you," he said, and then tailed off. "Life's been very complicated."

"How's the French tart in North Oxford?" I said as I carried on pulling books out of boxes.

He brightened suddenly.

> *"A nubile Parisian whore*
> *Courted courtiers stiff by the score*

She found their rigidity
Dispelled her frigidity
Reducing her mores to 'More!'"

I didn't smile at this and he unbrightened again.

"She went long ago," he said finally.

"You and Donna?"

"About as successful as you and Rachel. You don't drink anymore, I hear, or I'd invite you for—"

"No, Bill," I said. "I'm one of those who can't manage the odd drink. I'm either drunk or sober. These days I'm sober."

"Doesn't seem long ago, does it?"

"No," I said. "It doesn't."

"You don't even smoke, then?" he said, as he took out his cigarettes.

"No. Can't," I said. "One punctured lung and one . . . well, never mind. You can't smoke either, Bill. Not in here. The place is a tinderbox."

He went outside onto the Common and I watched him for a moment. I still admired the way he held that cigarette. I would have liked to join him.

The pictures started coming in from Mervyn's clientele. He had explained to them that this was not merely an exhibition, it was effectively an assessment of the man's life and work. Not to have one's work shown there might raise a question about its place in the oeuvre.

"Who's handling security?" he said.

"New York. The Archivist is coming over specially for the occasion. So Mrs. Simkins tells me."

"Who is he?"

"Nobody knows."

"Great. This gets better all the time. How did I ever come to be involved with the Delaquay Society anyway?"

"Greed, Mervyn," I said. "Probably your most likable trait. Certainly the most human one I've noticed. Your head's healed up nicely."

Mrs. Simkins brought me tea. She would often pour herself a sherry in the afternoon.

"You don't partake, I think?" she said, waving the bottle at me once. "It's only that I heard you talking to Mr. Blanchard . . ."

"No," I said. "I'm one of those who doesn't."

"My husband, God rest his soul, he shouldn't have done, you know. He had the weakness. But he couldn't stop. Obviously didn't have your willpower. Cirrhosis got him in the end. Mind you, he was very amusing in his drink. When he was capable of coherent speech, he could be very funny indeed."

It was strange to see those big volumes of the Proceedings come out of their wrappers. I was back again in Beaumont Street, turning those pages, drinking Bill's whiskey. That big bed. Donna. Rachel. Little by little we put the exhibition together, had the photographs taken, wrote the catalog. The only things we were missing were the contributions from New York. The exhibition was due to start on the Friday. The packages finally arrived on the Monday but without the man from New York.

I had never seen any of the works from the late period, though I had read more references to them than I could recall. Now here was his *Tempest* and his *St. John's Gospel.* I sat in the gallery into the evening that day looking at them, turning the pages back and forth in the same trance that I'd once known when I first saw the Milton. Whatever had happened in Delaquay's life had found a reconciling form in these late works. There was a tranquillity that hushed the page before you.

The drawing of Jesus healing the sick man was a self-portrait. Delaquay was the sick man but his face already showed the healing beginning. And the rubric changed against the words "Do you truly want to be well?" And in *The Tempest,* he portrayed himself as Trinculo, while Prospero commanded the waves. In the front of the Shakespeare he had written an inscription (to whom?):

Don't lament Milan.
Don't grieve for your lost kingdom.
Bless the thief for he lightens your burden.

Mrs. Simkins had come up behind me at one point and leaned over my shoulder as I looked at the illustrations.

"Those are lovely things," she said.

"Yes, they are."

"Some of the others in those books seem positively evil."

"He went a long way down, our Mr. Delaquay."

"How did he come back up?"

"I don't know," I said. "Shouldn't think anybody does."

28

Homecoming

Stand in the middle of a great city and remind yourself: the soft hands of man raised all this up and may one day take it down again.

ALFRED DELAQUAY, *Diaries*

BY THE DAY OF THE OPENING THE NEW YORK ARCHIVIST HAD still not arrived. We opened without him. It made a handsome collection. I had almost forgotten by the end how many my own hands had made. I would often walk over and pick up *The Tempest* when no one else was looking at it.

Peter turned up with Solly, who wore a leather mask through which the unburned part of his face and his one good eye peered out.

"Look at the pair of you," Peter said, shaking his head. "Just look at what you've done to yourselves."

"At least Solly's wounds served a purpose," I said.

"Did they?" Peter said. "I hadn't realized. The B-52's have stopped flying, then, have they?"

Solly squinted at him but said nothing. After they had walked around a few times, Solly came over to me.

"Some of this is extraordinary," he said. "I'd never realized he was such an important artist. That *Paradise Lost.* I'd give my right arm to own that."

"There's not enough of you left to give any more away, Sol," Peter said gently.

"It's yours, Solly. After the exhibition's over, I'll give it to you."

He looked at me skeptically.

"It's in my keeping," I said. "I'm entitled to pass it on if I choose."

"You're being serious?" he said.

"Yes. But to take it you'll have to accept the rules of the Society."

"What are they?"

I'd realized even as I said it.

"Forget it," I said. "The Society no longer has any rules. Do what you like with it."

"The man from Sotheby's valued that one at thousands of pounds," Sol said. "We heard him talking."

"What does he know?" I said. "These fellows wouldn't know a real Delaquay from a fake. How could they?"

Peter looked at me and smiled. "Maybe you should show them how," he said.

"Not yet," I said. "Let's enjoy the show."

Mervyn started out nervous, but as he heard the rumors of the rising Sotheby evaluations, his expression relaxed.

"It's going well," he said.

"Well, thank you, Mervyn. Maybe all my years at the Astley Gallery weren't entirely wasted, after all."

Bill and Donna arrived with young Tom. Not so young anymore. Bill had to be told to put out his cigarette before entering. The boy's physiognomy was no longer so ignoble. He was beginning to take after his father.

"It's very handsome, Tom," Bill said to me. None of us seemed too worried anymore about which hand any of this had come from.

I hadn't expected Rachel, though if I'd thought about it I might have done. Her hair was more gray now than brown. She didn't see me until she had been around all the rooms. I didn't want to interrupt her. Then she stopped at the desk. I could see the startled look in her eyes, but I'd seen that look so many times in so many faces I'd grown used to it. We walked outside on the Common.

"I heard you'd had a bad accident."

"Yes. I was on my way to see you, oddly enough."

She stopped again and looked at me.

"A real mess, eh?" I said.

"I've seen worse."

"People say that to me all the time. It's not as cheering as they seem to think."

"Half the things in there are by you."

"Quiet now!" I said. "Don't tell the nice man from Sotheby's that."

"What's it all for? What's the point of the exhibition, Tom?"

"Search me."

"I have to go. I have to get my train back to Oxford."

"Is there a man, Rachel?"

"There've been a few."

"If I applied to come back to the Lenau . . ."

"I'd certainly give you a reference," she said. "It would be reasonably good. Don't expect me to provide accommodation, though. But, then, you'd always be able to stay with Bill and Donna. Quite helpful for your research, I should think, on the topography of hell. And now hadn't you best go back to your party?"

"Party?"

"Whatever you call it. Whatever it is."

She still had that light step over the ground, throwing her shawl over one shoulder.

Mrs. Simkins was coming out of the gallery door. "It's wonderful," she said. "A wonderful way to hand over. There's a taxi been sent over. I have to leave a set of keys for the New York Archivist. They're being taken to his hotel, so they'll be there when he arrives. Exciting, isn't it?"

That night I sat in my flat in Paddington and flicked through the catalog. I didn't know what all this was for either. I couldn't answer Rachel's question. And yet I felt strangely exhilarated. I felt like drinking some champagne, but I was too frightened of what would come next.

The knock on the door came at about nine o'clock. When I saw him standing there, the strangest thing was that I felt no surprise at all, just a freakish sense of inevitability. It was me twenty-five years later if I hadn't smashed my face up. This was Thomas, son of Patrick and Agatha, and father of Thomas.

"The New York Archivist," I said. "Come in."

He sat in his long coat in the chair and looked at me.

"I heard about the accident," he said. "I'm sorry."

"Never learned to say father," I said. "What am I supposed to call you?"

"Call me Tom."

"I'd offer you a drink but I don't keep any."

"That's not a problem."

"You couldn't tell me why, could you?" I said, standing up and walking to the window. "Would you like to fill in some of the holes of the last thirty years that I've spent so much of my time falling into?"

He didn't move from the chair. He was still handsome. I could see what Donna saw in him.

"He had taught me to be as passionate about things as he was himself," he said. "My father. Your grandfather. Grimshaw. With my work in Germany, I was in touch with the underground movements there. The anti-Nazis. We felt . . . I'm afraid we felt the Church had disgraced itself. When the Fulda Declaration came out reversing the previous prohibitions on Roman Catholics being Nazis, we felt someone had to act.

"The *Hindenburg* was somehow the most important target. You probably can't understand it now, but it seemed to us they'd actually put the swastika into the skies. They'd taken heaven by force. We wanted to take it out again. No one was to be killed, Tom. The device was to explode on U.S. soil long after landing. We had planned an emergency call which would have cleared the hangars. The one thing we couldn't control was the weather.

"I was meant to be on the flight. That's the proof of it, when I say that no one was to be hurt. I would have been in the damned thing myself, but for the holdup getting there. One of the ground crew was with us. He'd already planted the device I'd given him the week before.

"Then the news came back. I was listed among the dead. To admit then that I'd not been on it would have made me the prime suspect and endangered the lives of the men and women we were working with. I made my way to New York and disappeared into the Delaquay Society. That was the easiest part. A man who was no one in a society that didn't exist."

"You could have let me know," I said.

"I couldn't let you know anything. Or your mother either. It would have made you vulnerable. All I could do was to check. Whatever her faults, she was at least good to you."

"She wasn't," I said, turning around at last and looking at him, with a face older than his own. "She was a miserable, vindictive, coldhearted bitch who resented every second of my childhood and seemed to blame me for your death."

His composure was unsettled for the first time. His eyes asked me to say it wasn't true. My eyes told him it was.

"Then I'm sorry," he said at last, and looked down at the floor. "Then I truly didn't understand."

"That makes two of us, not understanding."

"I tried to make arrangements so I could help in some way."

"You also had me thrown out of Beaumont Street."

"No, Tom, you had yourself thrown out of there."

"So what happens now?"

"I have a job to do here, then you won't see me again, I'm afraid."

"What is all this for? What's the point of the exhibition? Why have you bought the gallery? Who's going to run it? Nobody knows what's happening."

All the time as I looked at his face I felt as though I were looking into my own unscarred future.

"It will become clear soon enough," he said. He stood up to leave. "I'm sorry, Tom. Truly."

"You said that when you came in."

"Because it's true. You might not have been loved at close quarters, but believe me you were loved at a distance. And Patrick and Agatha adored you."

"I wasn't there when either of them died."

"I wasn't there when you were born. And you won't be there when I die either. There's no stranger family than ours."

He was gone. And I was left to sit at the table until dawn, staring out into the darkness, waiting for the stars to fade.

29

Jervaulx

*What is it that attracts the mind to ruins? There we gaze on
time's blank indifference to the makings of man.*
ISAAC LENAU, *Marginalia,* 1003

BY THE TIME I ARRIVED AT THE EDGE OF THE COMMON THE NEXT
day some of the fire engines were already on their way back to the station.
The Temple Gallery was now a smoldering black stain still crackling
across the grass. One or two withered uprights were standing, but it had
been an efficient fire. A few desultory arcs of water were still being
directed by a couple of firemen, but the real excitement was over. The fire
had destroyed the Temple, and now water had quenched the fire.

I began at last to understand.

"That's Mr. Lynch," shouted Mrs. Simkins as she saw me. "Oh, Mr.
Lynch, isn't this terrible? I can't imagine anything more terrible. Really
I can't."

The policeman asked if I could join him for a second. We sat on the
bench as he took out a notepad. All I could do was gaze over at the ooz-
ing, acrid mess that had contained the works of Alfred Delaquay the day
before.

"Do you know anything about this, sir?"

"How do you mean?"

"This was a deliberate fire, there's no question of that. Paraffin was
doused all over the building. A neighbor over there saw someone letting
himself in last night with a key."

"And you think it was me, do you?"

"No, sir, I don't, as a matter of fact. I checked that. The man who was seen had no . . . his legs were . . ."

"He wasn't a cripple," I said.

"You had one set of keys, sir," he went on. "Mrs. Simkins had another. The third I believe was sent to someone called . . ." Here he read out carefully, "the Archivist of the New York Delaquay Society. Do you know who that person might be?"

"No," I said, after thinking for a moment. "No, I'm afraid I don't. Introductions were kept to a minimum. Was anyone hurt?"

"What?"

"Was anyone hurt? In the fire."

"No. One of the officers has a strained wrist. They received a call, you see. Telling them the fire had started. That's the strange thing, or one of them. They must have been called out almost as soon as the blaze started, even though it was the middle of the night. But, of course, a wooden structure like that, it went up like a firework. Couldn't save anything from it. But Mrs. Simkins said she had the keys delivered over to the Dorchester Hotel yesterday for this Archivist fellow. The only person who checked in from America there yesterday was a Mr. Grimshaw, who is now untraceable. Nobody seems to know who he is.

"Do you know anyone called Grimshaw?"

"I did once," I said. "But you'd best take a shovel with you if you're planning on interviewing him."

I walked up and down over the charred smolder. There were little fragments of books and drawings, tiny slivers that escaped the fire. I recognized a piece of the vellum binding that had covered the Milton. I put it in my pocket. Solly would have to make do with that now.

Mervyn arrived, grim and white-faced.

"There's no insurance cover on any of it," he spat out at me. "I gave personal guarantees to bring this material here. I thought you said the New York group was arranging security?"

"They did," I said. "All the reputations are secure now, Mervyn. At least you won't have any awkward questions about provenance to answer."

"This will ruin me," he said. "I'll have to leave the country."

"You will take Donna with you, I hope. Your sister's very devoted to you, you know."

I kept walking up and down. The blackness gradually cooled beneath my feet. The smell turned heavy and sodden. It all fitted together, but I was astonished at the ruthlessness. Even the *St. John's Gospel* and *The Tempest.* Couldn't he have simply left them behind? Did everything have to go like this?

As the dark came in I saw his shape a few hundred feet away on the Common. A gray shadow beckoning me. I walked over casually.

"There isn't long, Tom, I must be leaving."

"All done then?"

"Yes. You understand now?"

"I suppose so. The point had been lost with Delaquay?"

"No. I think Delaquay made his point very well, don't you? Otherwise there wouldn't have been any need for this little fire."

"You got the timing right this time."

"This time."

"Didn't you keep anything?"

"No. There would be no point. Once greed and deceit had entered the Society, there was nothing else to do but destroy it."

"That's what the Reformers said, isn't it? That's why they left us all those ruins up in Yorkshire."

I turned back and looked at those smoky remains.

"The church of the four winds," I said. "I suppose it's what Grimshaw told me I could expect to inherit."

He placed an arm around my neck, as Bill used to do.

"Does he know? Blanchard, does he know that you're . . . ?"

"Now that Grimshaw's dead, no one knows but you."

"What will you do?" I said. "How will you live?"

"I have one advantage over you there, Tom," he said. "Remember that I learned how to be someone else a long time ago. Except for you, I don't even exist."

Acknowledgments

I would like to thank Philip Byrne, G. F. Dutton, David Elliott, Marius Kociejowski, and W. S. Milne for their astute readings and encouragement.

The generous allegiance of Elena Lappin was invaluable.

I am particularly indebted to Anthony Rudolf, whose work has many shadows in the text, as does that of Walter Benjamin and Aby Warburg.

A part of the narrative of Solomon Levine first appeared as a short story, "The Strange Case of Solomon Levine," in *The Jewish Quarterly*.